D1579912

They call themselves the Devil's Clan: to the occupying English army they are rebels outside the law, who can expect no mercy. For this is 1746. Bonnie Prince Charlie's dreams of restoring the Stuart monarchy lie shattered with his broken army on Culloden Moor, and the victors have begun their merciless campaign of terror. On a bloody rampage through the Highlands they slaughter men, women and children indiscriminately, raping, looting, cramming their jails with the wounded and laying the countryside to waste.

Alasdair MacDonald of Glencoe escaped from Culloden. Now with only three companions, he continues the fight. Their mission – the assassination of 'Butcher' Cumberland, commander of the English army and son of King George II. Their enemy – Captain Forbes Hinchcliffe, the ruthless sadistic Englishman who has vowed to see Alasdair in hell.

The Devil's Clan

ALEXANDER SCOTT

NEW ENGLISH LIBRARY
TIMES MIRROR

For my Mother

A New English Library Original Publication 1978
© by Alexander Scott 1978

*

FIRST NEL PAPERBACK EDITION FEBRUARY 1978

Conditions of sale: This book is sold subject to the condition that it shall not, by way of trade or otherwise, be lent, re-sold, hired out, or otherwise circulated without the publisher's prior consent in any form of binding or cover other than that in which it is published and without a similar condition including this condition being imposed on the subsequent purchaser.

NEL Books are published by
New English Library Limited from Barnard's Inn, Holborn, London EC1N 2JR
Made and printed in Great Britain by Hunt Barnard Printing Ltd., Aylesbury, Bucks.

45003399 6

Introduction

On the 25th of July, in the year of our Lord 1745, Prince Charles Edward Louis Phillipe Casimir Stuart landed in the Highlands of Scotland. He had come to claim the throne of England for his father, James the Old Pretender, son of the overthrown King James the Second of England. Many of the Clans were quick to follow their young Jacobite hero in rebellion against the Hanoverian King, George the Second, the 'wee German lairdie' then ruling Britain.

The Clans gathered in late August under the Prince's banner at Glenfinnan, and marched at once to Edinburgh, which they took with comparative ease. The increasingly confident army of 5,000 rebels then routed the English at Prestonpans and proceeded south through Carlisle, Manchester and Derby. London, largely unprotected, trembled at the approach of the 'wild savages'.

In one of the most curious actions in Britain's military history, Prince Charles, having been advised by his commanders, withdrew his army back over the Scottish border. Certainly the expected Jacobite support among the common people of Britain had not materialised, but London had lain wide open in front of him, ready to be conquered. Once the element of surprise which had swept them to early victory had gone, the Highlanders, despite a small victory at Falkirk, were finished.

By April 1746, William, Duke of Cumberland, son of King George, fresh from his successes in Flanders, had marched with an impressive army and was in control of Aberdeen. He moved in that month on Inverness, and, on the 16th of April, faced the Highland army across Culloden Moor. The battle that followed proved the beginning of the end for a proud and ancient race of warriors and a way of life that had survived for centuries.

Of the Highland Clans that marched behind the King, it was

the MacDonalds, former Lords of the Western Isles of Scotland and most powerful of the Clans, who formed the backbone of the rebellion, and on whom the English perpetrated their most hideous crimes after the battle of Culloden.

This is the story of Alasdair MacDonald, a member of the most notorious sept of Clan Donald, and his refusal to accept defeat.

CHAPTER ONE

THE HOMECOMING

A vicious wind howled down the length of Glencoe, buffeting between the parallel lines of black mountains that scowled down at the valley floor. At the eastern end of the Glen stood a small village made up of fourteen crude, mud-formed dwellings standing in a rough circle around a modest wooden house.

The village seemed dead save for a body now and then discernible through the swirling mists that scudded along the valley floor.

Angus MacDonald lay against one of the outer huts with his knees drawn up to his chin. Covered in a brown woman's shawl, a blue bonnet fitted with the white cockade of the Jacobites perched on his head, the gaunt boy looked oddly younger than his thirteen years as he lay there like some discarded rag doll. He dozed fitfully, his hand raised occasionally to brush away the fierce Highland midges searching for warmth in the folds of his tattered clothing.

Charged with keeping watch from three o'clock until dawn, exhaustion had overtaken him with a few minutes to go. A proud young man, his eyes had glistened keenly when old Duncan, his grandfather, had granted him the most important watch of all. He had sworn to lose a limb rather than fail in his duty, thinking that his father would indeed be proud of him on his return from battle, and would truly be able to call his son a man.

In the hours before he had succumbed to sleep, Angus had been mulling over the strange events that had caused a guard to be set in the first place.

Two days before, in the middle of the villagers' meagre midday meal, Angus's young cousin, Millie, was sent to find out what was upsetting the cattle lowing and shuffling near the village. She rushed back seconds later, flushed and shouting excitedly. Duncan threw down his bread, tired of her incoherent gabblings, and hobbled outside.

Lying on the earth in front of the house was a Highlander, though hardly recognisable as such. He was without his plaid, and his kilt and jacket were torn to shreds. His ravaged face was covered in cuts and dirt, and his eyes, as they looked up, were deeply haunted. He stared at the old man in front of him and moved his mouth as if trying to speak, but no sound came forth. Duncan, seeing the man's plight, knelt as quickly as his aged body would allow and placed his ear close to the man's mouth. He listened for a moment and gasped.

The Highlander's voice had been quiet and hoarse, but the words had been quite distinct.

'If you are Duncan MacDonald of Glencoe, your son lies dead at Culloden.'

Duncan's gnarled hands shot forward and grasped what was left of the man's jacket.

'You lie to me, you dog!' he shouted, shaking him violently until the Highlander's eyes rolled upwards and his head went limp.

Duncan stopped at length and knelt there, breathing hard, composing himself. His breath formed small jets of steam.

By now, all the people of the village had crowded into the square in front of the house, women and children in the main. Duncan addressed himself to them without turning round.

'Drag this dog into the house. Wake him, give him food. Bathe him if necessary. Just give him the wits to talk. I have a great many questions to ask the scoundrel. Do it now. At once!' Two black-shrouded women scuttled towards the body.

After two hours they had brought him round. The villagers stood breathless, watching him eat. He ate like a man who had not seen food for many days. He tore into the bread, chunks of it falling into the hands of the young children crouched at his feet. At length he drew his cuff across his overstuffed mouth and sat back, momentarily sated now looking more like the Highlander that he was. He had been washed, his cuts tended and his new clothes, though ill-fitting, were an improvement on the foul-smelling, blood and sweat-stained rags in which he had first appeared before them.

'Thank you, kind people. I was near dead of hunger.'

'We are not grown fat ourselves,' muttered one of the women cradling a skinny infant in her arms.

'Quiet, woman,' scolded Duncan. 'Never let it be said we forget our hospitality.'

The girl blushed and cast her eyes downwards.

'Now, sir,' Duncan turned to his guest. 'Hospitality or no, you have some explanations to make. You tell me my son is dead.'

'A thousand apologies, sir, for distressing you in such a fashion.' The Highlander's voice was still weak, and the people in the dark, wooden room had to strain to catch his words, but the hoarseness had gone and his Gaelic once more had the soft lilt common to that tongue. 'I was near to fainting and had not my wits about me.'

'Huisht man, enough footling around.' Duncan's voice was urgent. 'Is my son dead? Tell me at once.'

The Highlander's eyes darted uncomfortably. 'Although I did not see him die . . . '

'Ah, now we hear the truth!'

The Highlander halted for a moment, unwilling to hurt his host. At length he continued. 'If he is alive, it is a miracle.'

'They have been known to happen in these parts,' interjected an old man standing near the front of the crowd.

'Here they might happen, but not, I fear, at Culloden Moor.'

'How Culloden?' asked Duncan. 'What would my son be doing at such a God-forsaken place?'

The Highlander took a deep breath. ''Tis there we fought the English.'

A series of gasps punctuated his simple statement.

'I hear you all start,' he continued, 'but it is the truth. Why should I tell you different?'

'You could be a Campbell come to assess our strength.' One of the old men stepped forward. 'I still remember the Massacre when those Campbell bastards cut us down. Our guests they were, and they rose in the night to kill us like dogs. How do we know you are not one of that crew?'

The Highlander turned to face the old man and with eyes sparkling said, 'Sir, I am a MacDonald from Skye. I can trace my ancestry back to the Lords of the Isles. I shall do so now, if you do not believe me!'

This announcement was greeted with amazement by the crowd. The Highlander turned to Duncan, still angry. 'How would I have got into the state you saw me in had I been a spy?'

Duncan looked thoughtfully at him before speaking.

'True enough, sir. And you would not claim to be able to trace your ancestry unless you could do it. No man can learn

9

such a feat unless it is his heart's pride to do so. Continue, MacDonald of Skye.'

The Highlander stared for a moment at the table surface before resuming. 'It was late in the morning of the fifteenth day of this month we prepared for battle. The rain poured down. We stood up to our ankles in mud. Some of us were sick and found it hard to control our bowels. Others shivered violently, cold sweat glistening on their faces. Many had made a forced march to surprise the English camp at Nairn that very night. It came to naught. Few of us had eaten for three days. I had not slept for four, but my heart swelled with pride once more as midday approached. For all our hardships and the ravages of desertion, there were still some thousand members of Clan Donald on the left flank of the Prince's army. There must have been near 5,000 members of other clans besides us, but I was only interested in the MacDonalds. For a strange moment I felt that we had returned to do battle behind the Lord of the Isles, but my romantic notions soon dispersed amid the grumbling of my fellows.'

He paused, sipping at a glass of whisky which Duncan had poured for him.

'In the minutes before battle many doubts were raised. Why were we, Highlanders, facing the English on flat ground with nary a boulder nor a tree to protect us? It was as if our commanders had chosen a battlefield as like to the Englishmen's playground, Flanders, as possible. Cumberland, my comrades assured me, would laugh to face us on these terms. I scoffed at them, calling them cowards for voicing such opinions. Did they not remember, I asked them, our success at Falkirk, where the English ran like frightened puppies before us?'

He shook his head slowly.

'I would deliver my heart fresh beating from my body to take back my foolish words. I swear that some of our men were ready to bolt for safety, but then our Chiefs came riding before us. The three leaders of Clan Donald came separately – Clanranald, Glengarry and then Keppoch, his face a terrifying sight. He had argued with the Prince to get us our rightful place on the right flank – as you know it has been the prerogative of the MacDonalds for centuries to take that flank – and he had lost. He glowered at us, and I am not afraid to admit that his look stirred my bowels afresh. I would rather have fought a hundred English than face him at that moment.'

The Highlander smiled ruefully at the thought.

'He spoke quietly as he rode in front of us, and said but one thing to all. "Remember who you are this day and for what you fight." We understood and our backs stiffened.' The Highlander sighed and took another sip of his whisky.

'I am a simple warrior, when I'm not stealing cattle or tending my crops, and have no way of describing the broad events of the battle until our poets write it for me, if we have poets left! The fighting started on the right, where we should have been. Lochiel's men from Lochaber, the Camerons, bore the brunt, with Stewarts from Appin and members of Clan Fraser. They almost broke the English but the southern troops showed more resolve than one would have credited them. There was much hand fighting before they were driven back. So our right was defeated. Then our centre, Clan Chattan and the Farquharsons, attacked, but again they were driven back in disarray. Only then did the MacDonalds attack. I knew at once how right my companions had been. Before we advanced to within forty yards of their line, their guns cut us to shreds. Blood spurted over me. The men to the left and right of me, cousins both, died screaming, one with his face blown away, the other clutching his stomach. Those of us who were left stood facing the English. We were like madmen. I had my claymore and dirk in my hand and screamed and snarled at the guns but knew not what to do.'

His speech came more quickly as his narrative continued: 'I could see the English through the smoke despite the blood that covered my face. Some of them were laughing. The gorge rose in my throat and I raced towards them, stumbling over the bodies of those who had tried to reach them already. Within thirty yards of the line, grape shot entered my arm. I did not notice it until my hand loosened its grip on my claymore, and then I looked down and saw the terrible mess. I fell to the ground, clutching the wound, trying to stem the flow.

'As I knelt there, a young man ran screaming past me. I can still hear his chilling call: "We are sons of dogs come for meat." I could see some of the English look apprehensively at this figure. His fury, I admit, would have alarmed me had I been facing him. I shouted after him: "Kill them, kill the dogs," as he raced towards them. How he was not hit by rifle shot, I cannot tell. As he reached their line, he raised the claymore high above his head and cleft the man in front to the navel, but the next redcoat in the line bayoneted him in

11

the side. My brave friend thanked the soldier by severing his head with one blow.

'He crawled slowly back to where I lay and collapsed by me. He must have seen that my wound was not serious, for he said:

"I am dying. Get word to my father, Duncan MacDonald of Glencoe that I died valiantly for the Prince. Tell him to get our family to France. Do you understand me? Then get up and run, man! Enough of our clan has perished in this mad venture." I struggled to my feet and stopped to pick him up, but he shouted that he would kill me if I did not leave, so I left him and started running. My horse lies dead outside your village. How his heart lasted so far, I do not know. It is no less surprising that I am here myself.'

The Highlander, whose eyes had been fixed on the rough table in front, as he relived the horror of the battle, shifted his gaze to Duncan's face. The old man was holding back tears.

'I am sorry, Duncan MacDonald, to have brought you such terrible news. I fear it will become a common duty to me when I return to my own island. Please take your son's advice. Leave for France. Louis will give us better protection than Prince Charlie could.'

The old man, swiftly changing mood as old men often will, became angry: 'I warn you, sir, I shall not hear treason spoken in my house. If I had been ten years younger, I would gladly have fought for the Prince. Aye, and I would gladly have died for him too.'

He looked meaningfully at the warrior.

'Are you calling me a coward, sir?'

'We know our duty. That is all I will say.'

The Highlander took a deep breath.

'I will excuse you, old man. It is grief talking. I will tell you one thing, however, that might help to change your opinion of our glorious leader. As I left the field, a man ran with me. He told me that the Prince had left the battle soon after its commencement. As he ran, crying, an officer called out to him, "Go on, run, you cowardly Italian." The Prince made no reply. Could a true Highland leader have left unpunished such a remark?'

'I shall not pass comment, sir. I forgot myself. It was kind and courageous of you to come here. I do not doubt your bravery, believe me.'

'Then gather your possessions, sir, and come with me. I will take my family to France, and you shall sail with us if you so desire.' The warrior rose to his feet. 'I can wait no longer. It is still a long journey to Skye. You may not get another chance, I warn you.'

The old man stared at him for a few moments. One of the younger women approached him and whispered something in his ear. He shook his head slowly and dismissed her before continuing:

'We cannot accompany you to France, sir. I will not believe that my son is dead. I have given him up as lost too many times in the past to doubt him now.' The old man's chin was set in an attitude of stubborn defiance.

The warrior's eyes filled with tears of compassion.

'You are a brave man. I hope to God that your faith is justified. Only hope sustains us now.' As he stood, unsteady on his feet, breathing heavily, still weak from his journey, others in the hut approached him and asked for news of the other young men who had accompanied their leader to war.

'I am afraid I did not know your kinsmen,' he replied softly with a sad shake of his head. 'I will pray for them with all my heart.'

He made his way to the door where he paused for a moment. Without looking round, he spoke:

'These are bad times for us. There has already been great bloodshed, and the glens will run with blood for months to come. But we will repay the English and the Lowlanders one day. It will need one man with enough courage to rise from our beaten ranks. He will come though . . . and soon. I feel it. I feel it in my bones. Vengeance will be ours!'

He straightened his back and strode from the house.

Duncan turned to Angus. 'Go after him and give him one of our horses. The beasts are no longer strong, but one of them will at least carry him up the Glen to Loch Leven.'

He bade his crestfallen people leave him and, as they shuffled out, he poured himself whisky and began to plan.

He would not give up his son for dead until he saw the boy's body before him. In the meantime he would organise a Watch just in case things were as bad as the warrior had suggested. There were nineteen people left in the village, but they were mostly women – sturdy women, it was true, but no match for British troops. They could take the Day Watch. The Night Watch would have to be divided between himself and old John

13

MacDonald, his constant companion of many years. Could Angus be trusted with the responsibility of sharing the Watch with them? There was little choice, and he was a brave young lad, with many of his father's qualities. He might need them now, Duncan grimly reflected.

According to their visitor, the battle had taken place three days before. He would give his son another week, and then if necessary, would set out to find him.

The old man crossed himself quickly.

Glencoe is an eight-mile long scar in the ground running from east to west along northern Argyllshire on Scotland's western seaboard. A fertile though melancholy place, it is bounded on the south by Bidean nam Bian, the highest mountain in the shire, topped by five separate knuckles that eternally threaten the sky above. Along the northern edge of the Glen runs Aonach Eagach, a sharp-toothed escarpment that glares across, hunched and jagged, at the mountains opposite. In the west the valley runs into the inviting waters of Loch Leven, and into the danger-filled wastes of Rannoch Moor in the east.

The village in which Angus MacDonald slept was situated at the eastern end of the Glen, close to Rannoch, and nestled in the dark shadows of Aonach Eagach, the Notched Ridge.

All of the many high passes leading from the valley to north and south will lead the unsuspecting stranger to high mountains, with no choice but to return and start once more. All, that is, except one. From Kinlochleven, at the eastern end of Loch Leven, which winds round behind the Notched Ridge, it is possible to descend into Rannoch Moor and turn into Glencoe, but it is a dangerous route, requiring the traveller to hug the escarpment wall for five painful miles before reaching the Moor. The route is known with good reason as the Devil's Staircase.

Alasdair MacDonald, severely wounded in the side and with four days of continuous hard travel behind him, had been forced to undertake the last part of his journey, the hardest, on foot, his horse having collapsed with exhaustion before reaching the top of the pass. The Devil's Staircase had almost killed him.

Blood still trickled from the wound in his side where a redcoat's bayonet had speared him. His jacket, plaid, kilt, all were stained in a sickly dark-red mixture of blood and dirt. His legs and arms, where they were bare through his torn jacket, were covered in cuts and scratches. Only the eyes were clearly visible in his mud-encrusted face.

At the foot of the Staircase one can either descend into Rannoch Moor and then into Glencoe, or hug the escarpment wall and end up overlooking the Glen itself. Dimly realising that he had at best an hour of consciousness at his disposal, Alasdair had chosen the latter course. Difficult as the journey along the Staircase had been, it was made to seem a stroll along a city street compared with the journey along the escarpment. Somehow through his sweat and pain, he crawled, crablike along the wall until he came to a flat clearing which, Alasdair remembered, overlooked his village. He smiled to himself faintly in the dark and began the climb down to the arms of his family. Within a few yards his legs, taxed beyond endurance, lost all strength and buckled beneath him. He fell, his hands grasping vainly in the blackness of the night. He plummeted forward, his body bouncing off the craggy stone of the escarpment, each bump forcing the air from his lungs until smashing against a jagged clump of rock that violently halted his fall. Had it not been for the fact that his plaid had somehow twisted itself around his head in the descent, his skull would have split in two. There he lay for hours, unconscious, as death crept slowly through his body.

Perhaps Alasdair MacDonald had been meant for greater things for during that chill night something close to a miracle took place. When death had almost overtaken him, life ebbed back into his body, slowly at first, and then as dawn came, with a surge that caused him to awaken. His eyes flickered open, but all was dark around him. 'Am I blind?' he muttered, fighting the terror that whispered to him that he was beyond the grave. His panic mounted until he felt the plaid against his cheek. He tried to move his head, but pain shot through his skull. Slowly he tested his arms. One of them lay crooked in front of his face. He dragged the plaid away and blinked. He was staring down at the village, about 150 yards below. Across the valley the first light of dawn glinted on the knuckles of Bidean nam Biam.

With an effort he took a deep breath only to find it stifled by the violent wind.

Slowly he turned his head away and breathed again, deeply, trying to clear his head. When he looked back, a familiar scene lay before him, but his home and his mountains, lit by the leaden light of dawn and seen through eyes blurred by the wind, seemed dreamlike. Perhaps, he reflected, he had not been wrong; perhaps he had died and this was to be his last view of his homeland. He drank in the scene eagerly, rubbing his eyes with his hands.

Almost immediately he gasped. On the outskirts of the village lay a body wrapped in a brown shawl. It seemed to be a young boy, although it was difficult to tell from so far away. Could it be Angus? Alasdair's heart began a rapid beat. He called out, but the wind once more almost choked him and the cry carried far up the valley.

His joy turned to gnawing fear.

From behind the hut against which Angus lay crept a red-coated soldier. He approached the boy, pulled out a knife, leant down, grasped the boy's hair, jerked the head up and swiftly slit the exposed throat. The child jackknifed to attention, body rigid, his mouth moving desperately to form a sound that would never come. As he choked to death, the soldier calmly wiped the blade of his knife on the quickly reddening shawl.

From behind the huts which formed the boundary of the village on its northern side streamed a further dozen soldiers. They scuttled like red spiders across the village yard and disappeared into the huts around the main house. For a moment the village once more looked deserted, except for one man. A Captain of Horse, distinguishable by his elegant blue and gold-brocaded uniform, sauntered to the middle of the yard and stood, his hand resting upon his hip, a disdainful sneer marring his handsome features. He listened attentively to the screams that rent the air and mingled with the howls of the wind, as he fingered his pistol. From the hut to the right of the main house ran old John MacDonald. He was naked. Blood pouring from an ugly gash in his forehead blinded him. The Captain watched him until he had almost reached the shelter of the huts across the yard. Taking out his pistol he took careful aim, and shot the old man in the back. John's thin arms flew into the air as he dropped to the ground, where he lay writhing, face down. The Captain marched briskly to where he lay and aimed the pistol at his head. John's skull exploded and bone and flesh spattered unevenly for yards around.

The Captain grinned.

16

From the main house ran a woman, young and attractive, holding a sheet in front of her to hide her full-bodied nakedness. Her eyes bulged with fear as she dashed from the house followed by two laughing soldiers. Desperate, she ran straight into the arms of the waiting Captain who held her struggling form with little effort. He spoke sharply to the two soldiers who had followed her, and they turned away, obviously displeased at being robbed of their prey.

The Captain led the screaming woman by the wrists and pushed her roughly into the nearest hut, stepping over John's body. He followed her inside eagerly, his face twisted in lustful anticipation.

Outside the soldiers were slowly emerging into the daylight, clutching sheets, boxes, tankards and bottles. From one of the huts came two soldiers, one gripping an old woman by the arm, the other a young child, a boy of no more than six years of age. The old woman was thrown roughly to the ground. One of the soldiers knelt with his knee on her throat while another grabbed her hand. She struggled weakly as he tried to remove a ring from one of her fingers. When the soldier's efforts became more frantic, the Captain appeared from the hut and pushed his way through his men. He uttered a sharp order and the redcoat looked up at him, confused. The Captain repeated the order, drew out his knife and tossed it on the ground. The soldier picked it up and studied it. After a few seconds he let go of the old woman's arm and got up.

The Captain took two strides towards his subordinate, plucked the knife from his grasp, and knelt down beside the old woman, who now looked close to death, took her hand in his and with a clean, neat well-practised cut sliced off the finger which bore the ring. Blood spurted from the wound and the old lady let out a chilling scream that echoed down the valley. The Captain stood up, pocketed the whole finger and wiped the blade of his knife on the nearest soldier's tunic.

Suddenly the young boy who had been dragged out with the old woman, twisted out of his captor's grasp and rushed towards her body, but blundered into the Captain's legs and fell to the ground, crying. The boy crawled to the old lady, who had died from shock, and clung to her bosom, sobbing. The Captain motioned to one of the redcoats who walked to the boy and lifted him off the ground with one hand, taking out a bayonet with the other. With a chuckle, the soldier raised the tiny body into the air and slit along the underside of the child's belly and then threw the infant's body across that of the old woman.

Above, Alasdair watched frozen in horror and disbelief. This was a cruel dream. It could not be happening. Perhaps this was the first punishment of the afterlife. But no! This was reality and below his family was being slaughtered while he lay, powerless to help. It was a sickening irony.

His eyes burned into the Captain. He would meet him some-day this hound from hell, and would send him back to his master with his tail between his legs. He knew that he had seen him before, but where? His brain whirled as he watched the Captain walk towards the trooper who had been unable to carry out his barbaric order. The Captain knocked the young soldier to the ground and began kicking him repeatedly. The other soldiers did not watch, but stood shuffling nervously, their eyes avoiding the ugly scene.

A knife pressed against Alasdair's throat, and a knee was thrust into the small of his back.

'Stay still, or you die.'

CHAPTER TWO

THE ALLIANCE

A huge hand gripped Alasdair's chest and pulled him roughly on to his back.

He found himself staring into the eyes of James McIan, nephew to the leader of all the MacDonalds of Glencoe.

'Alasdair! I thought you were a Campbell.'

'McIan! Are you mad? How could I be a Campbell with the white cockade in my bonnet?'

'There's no bonnet on your head, you foolish man.'

' 'Tis you'll look foolish with my claymore through your liver.'

McIan stared down at Alasdair for a moment and emitted a laugh.

'We argued enough in the past. Surely we can be united now?' His huge, cheerful face, half-hidden by a flaming red beard, grew suddenly serious.

Alasdair remembered with a start what was happening below. He tried to twist on to his front.

'What are you doing?' McIan asked.

'Put me on my belly, McIan. My family is slaughtered below and I lie here squabbling with you.' The burly Highlander bent down at once and turned his companion over as easily as if he had been a feather. McIan, following Alasdair's gaze, gasped.

'My God, is that Angus and Old John down there?' Alasdair's head nodded faintly in assent as he tried to choke back tears.

McIan put a hand on Alasdair's shoulder in a clumsy gesture of compassion. 'Cry away, man, there's no one to see you.' McIan's voice was husky with emotion.

Alasdair broke into wracking sobs as he pressed his face against the cold, black stone of Aonach Eagach.

The troops were now ready to ride off. One of them had been dispatched to fetch the Captain's horse which stood grazing some fifty yards from the village. As they stood idly around, each individual checked his haul. The Captain took the old woman's finger from his pocket and attempted to prise the ring loose with his knife.

One of the soldiers with less booty to count than the rest, gazed up at the sky and whistled softly to himself. His eyes wandered over the impressive valley, absorbing the scenery so different from the hovel in Whitechapel which had formerly been his home.

Something moved on the escarpment. Two shapes. The soldier let out a cry and pointed at the figures. 'Look! Look!'

The Captain swung round, screaming the order to fire. In the seconds it took for the troops to load muskets and take aim, McIan had bent down, scooped Alasdair in his arms and had run off at a gallop along the wall of the escarpment, sending broken stone hurtling to the ground below. The first shots missed by inches. Before a second volley could be unleashed, McIan had reached one of the numerous passes leading out of the valley to high mountains. To the troops below chasing up the steep slope, it seemed as if the figures had disappeared into thin air. They had seen the Highlanders run for about a hundred yards along the slope, and then turn into a pathway leading directly upwards . . . and then they had vanished. The troops stopped in their tracks, uncertain of what to do. Their Captain's voice called up to them.

'I'll have you flogged at once if you don't follow, you miserable scum. After them!'

They began running once more until they reached the spot where the Highlanders had disappeared.

A tapering path led upwards and out of sight, with no sign of a hiding place except for one flattish boulder in the middle of the path behind which no normal man could hope to remain undetected, let alone the giant they had been firing at.

Presently their Captain appeared, his fashionable boots slipping against the hard, black stone.

His breath came in short gasps.   'Well . . . Where are they? . . . dogs . . . have you flogged.'

One of the soldiers stepped forward. It was the young trooper the Captain had punished minutes earlier. His face was beginning to puff out in ugly blue-black mounds.

'Captain, they've disappeared.'

'I can see that, you oaf, but where?'

His eyes searched around.

20

'Have you tried shifting the boulder?'

His men stood silent, embarrassed.

He walked up to it and beckoned forward two of the troops. 'Shift it.'

Heaving and straining, they managed to move the stone a few inches to the side.

The Captain motioned for others to help. Finally, with six men heaving, it slid aside to reveal a passage which led straight down for a few feet before turning to the side. It was large enough for two men. The Captain grinned. 'I think you'll find the rebel scum cowering in there. Go after them . . . No, wait. Let's amuse ourselves. You! Fetch wood from the village. We'll smoke them out.'

Presently smouldering wood was dropped into the hole by soldiers relieved at not having to brave the passage themselves.

After waiting for several minutes for two coughing figures to emerge from the hole, the Captain became bored and sent a man below to fetch some whisky from the main house and brandy from his own saddlebags. If the rebels had suffocated, there would be a long wait for the smoke to clear sufficiently to allow his men in to drag the bodies out.

The Captain smiled, imagining the discomfort of the trapped rats. He wondered if it was indeed Alasdair MacDonald down there. That would please him greatly.

A cry from below startled him from his reflections. The trooper sent to fetch the whisky had stopped some fifty yards below and was gesticulating wildly, pointing at something further up the valley. The Captain raced down the pass towards him, panic mounting in his breast.

About one hundred yards away, halfway up the escarpment, smoke was pouring from the mountain, as if from half-doused fire. But it was no fire.

A cold sensation gripped the Captain's stomach and a cry of anguish escaped from his lips. Duped, made to look foolish, and if he was not much mistaken, by that damned MacDonald again.

He swore to meet Alasdair MacDonald of Glencoe one day. He would enjoy watching him die.

About a mile up the valley Alasdair and Jamie lay panting, the thick heather cold, wet and reassuring against their backs.

The wind had subsided and the only sound was their rasping breath.

'Thank you, friend,' gasped Jamie. 'You saved us there. To have such an escape at the ready. Aye, you are a sly devil, even for a MacDonald.' He chuckled.

'My grandfather built it when he quarrelled with your family. He always feared that the McIans would one day take it upon themselves to drive us from the valley. Much of it is a natural passage. We had only to extend it a few yards to provide a method of escape in bad times.'

'For once, I am mighty pleased that our families have not always seen eye to eye.'

They turned their heads to smile at each other.

'Anyway,' Alasdair continued presently. ' 'Twas your big hairy arms which saved the day. For once I am glad you are twice the size of any normal man.'

They laughed, each pleased to have found a companion at such a desperate time. For a moment Alasdair even managed to forget the terrible scene he had witnessed, but after several minutes of silence his face grew sad once more.

'I must return to my people at once . . . if any of them are still alive.'

'But first we'll let the redcoats go about their evil business. I think they will move on across Rannoch. They must have come up from Fort William in the North and crossed Loch Leven at Invercoe before coming up the Glen. They will not want to return the same way.'

Alasdair interrupted. 'What about your family, McIan? Will they be safe?'

'Aye. We left them with adequate arms to see off any soldiers. They will be quite safe. It is almost as if the English are after your hide. There is no particular reason to wreak havoc here.'

'They have no cause to favour me with their cruelty. Yet I recognise that Captain from somewhere but I cannot recall where. It will come to me when we meet face to face!' Alasdair's lips met in a thin, determined line. 'Will you help me back to my home now? By the time we get there the troops should have moved on.'

'Of course, my friend, of course.'

Despite McIan's offer to carry him, Alasdair insisted on walking on his own legs, clinging to the crook of the huge Highlander's arm with one hand.

22

Presently they threw themselves down at a stream which trickled down the mountainside to feed the River Coe, and washed their faces, arms and legs as best they could, taking huge gulps of the clear water. Alasdair felt stronger and more capable of facing the ordeal that lay immediately ahead.

When they arrived the village seemed deserted once more. The soldiers had moved on, either up the Devil's Staircase or across Rannoch's treacherous wastes.

Alasdair walked between the huts, stunned and shocked almost beyond emotion. Death had been his companion for days now but had not prepared him for these sights.

He released his grasp on Jamie's arm, his own pain forgotten, and stumbled across to Angus's body. He knelt down by the boy, who now seemed to be sleeping, the terrible wound at his throat shadowed by his chin. He had been a proud boy, and Alasdair had loved him. They had been very much alike in many ways, and each day Alasdair noted with pride similarities: the child had been stubborn, unyielding, wilful, but with kindness and gentleness quite clearly marked in his character. Angus would have grown to resemble his father physically as well. Long eyelashes hiding piercing blue eyes, a strong, etched nose and soft full-lipped mouth. Alasdair reached out his hand to touch the boy's strangely blond hair. It pleased him to see his son as a throwback to the Vikings that had once ruled the Western Isles, and Angus had often shown himself to be as fearless a fighter and as proud of his honour as any Norseman.

Thirteen years old and dead for a cause he probably never understood.

Alasdair rose stiffly, weariness etched in his face. He moved to the main house . . . his house. Inside all was chaos. Heaps of rags and broken pottery littered the floor of the main hall. A groan came from the corner of the living room. It was his father. The old man was obviously dying. Alasdair raced to his side and raised the shrivelled old body in his arms.

'Father, it is me, Alasdair, your son. For God's sake wake up. You cannot die!'

The old man's eyes flickered open and a glint of recognition crept into them. 'Alasdair.' The voice was weak, faint, as if reaching back from another world. 'The miracle, it happened. You came. I was right.' The eyes glazed over and the blood drained from his cheeks. He stared lifelessly up at his son. Alasdair brought his hand softly over the eyelids and lay the body down gently before walking slowly from the house. In the

23

square stood three old ladies huddled together, seemingly the sole survivors. They looked like toys compared with Jamie who stood beside them, his huge hands around their slender shoulders.

One of the old black-clad trio detached herself from McIan's kindly grasp, and walked hesitantly towards Alasdair, who stood blinking in the daylight, unsure of where he was. Silently she gripped his hand and led him across the courtyard to one of the huts. Alasdair dimly recognised what was left of John's body. The old woman looked up at him and pointed to the low doorway.

Alasdair, bewildered, bent down and entered. He was hunched for a moment as the low ceiling would not allow him to stand. As his eyes grew accustomed to the darkness, he could just make out a form crouched by the far wall. Faint sobbing sounds reached his ears. He spoke, and the loudness of his voice startled him. 'Who are you?'

The sobbing stopped, and all was silence. Suddenly the form sprang to life and bolted for the door.

Alasdair's arm shot out and his hand grasped at the fleeing figure. The body did not stop and dragged him along with it through the door.

The person halted as if startled by the daylight. He was holding on to the arm of a naked woman. It was his wife.

She stared at him as if scrutinising a ghost, and then all at once fell into his arms where he held her with all of his depleted strength.

'Kathy, Kathy, my darling,' he murmured into her ear. 'You are safe. Thank God all is not lost.'

They stood there, rooted to the ground, he pouring words of love into her ear and stroking the jet-black hair that cascaded down her back, and she sobbing, her arms clasped around him as if her life now depended on keeping him by her, or as if she suspected him of being a phantom who would vanish were she to loosen her hold. At length they moved their heads back to look into each other's eyes.

'Oh, husband. Is this a dream?' Her voice was husky with emotion.

'Nay, my love. The nightmare is ended. I am here.'

He smiled reassuringly. She was even more beautiful than he remembered, with her delicate face, eyes warm and green like emeralds glinting in the sun, her flaring nostrils and rich, full mouth. He led her gently to the main house and noted with

24

odd amusement that McIan had turned his back on them, whether overcome with emotion or embarrassment at his wife's nakedness, Alasdair could not tell.

Once inside she turned to her husband, but could not meet his eyes. 'That man . . . ' she faltered. 'He . . . defiled me. I feel unclean.'

Alasdair caught her by the chin and raised her head.

'The Devil himself could not stain your purity. Not one hundred English troops. We shall mention it no more while we are together. Will you agree?'

She nodded her head in vigorous assent, her eyes burning passionately into his.

Two days later, his father and son properly buried with Catholic ritual, Alasdair sat in the main hall of old McIan's house in Invercoe, the traditional seat of MacDonald leaders in Glencoe.

The old chief, Jamie's uncle, had returned some two hours previously with half a dozen weary warriors having lost twelve men from his immediate family. Now he sat in front of the gigantic fireplace that provided heat in the dark winter months. The Chief turned to Alasdair, to whom he had been listening. His normally fierce countenance softened as he appraised the young man. He stroked his white beard, drawing it to a point and letting it spray out again before resuming. 'I cannot agree to do as you request, Alasdair, and before you ask, it has nothing to do with the bad feeling that has existed between our families since my father and your grandfather fell out. That is buried, as they both are. Oh, we have had our differences, you and I, and I dare say we will have more, but we have always relied on each other in times of trouble. We are, after all, members of Clan Donald. I am your Chief.' A harsh note had crept into the voice. He silenced an attempted interruption from Alasdair with a wave of the hand. 'The clans are dead. Their backbone lies shattered at Culloden. The Highlands will never again be what they once were. We have been beaten. We are warriors who live by the law of the sword. Well, the sword has spoken. We must accept its pronouncement.'

He rose from his seat and began to move towards the door, but Alasdair leapt in front of him, unable to contain his anger. The old man glared at him.

'Hear me this once, McIan. My grief entitles me to that privilege.' In new clothes, with body cleaned, wounds dressed and a claymore once more dangling from his belt, he looked but a distant relation to the man who had stumbled into the Glen only forty-eight hours before.

'I ask you to give me men to hunt the English dogs that slaughtered my family and raped my wife. If the Campbells had done this to one of your clansmen, you would not have thought twice about the need for revenge. You say we must accept the rule of the English, that you must consider your family. Good God, do you really believe they will let you live because you offer no resistance? You, the most feared and respected – some would say despised – leader of all the septs of our clan. You, direct descendant of those Lords of the Isles who paid no attention to English kings, let alone the German one under whom we now labour. You, descended from the great warrior Fingal that rid these glens of the heathen northmen. You are the worst enemy of the English. When you hear what they do to women and children, what do you think they will do to you, who led your men at Culloden?'

The words were now pouring from Alasdair.

'Perhaps we are dead. Perhaps we are ghosts that have not yet realised it, but I will not lay down and die for some up-start German. No, not for King George or for his bloated son. That filthy butcher Cumberland will see you drawn and quartered for his vile amusement. They will probably feed hunks of your flesh to the starving dogs that follow the camp. And they'll laugh while they do it. So join me now. Let us die with our heads high in battle.'

The old man raised his hand above his head and brought it down with stunning force on Alasdair's cheek.

'You dog,' he spluttered. 'You impudent young dog. You dare to tell me how to die, he who fought in battles before you were born, that protected you and your damn family a hundred times. If your family had not defied mine and if it had not been so unbending, you would not have had to live at the end of the Glen, a perfect target for all your enemies. You and your father and his damn father brought all this on your own heads. It was your pride that did it, and it is your pride that will ruin you now, you wretch.'

Alasdair interjected as the old man sought for words in his fury: 'Aye, and it is my pride that will not let me die like a

26

coward. I will not have my skin saved in order to behave as a sheep.'

The old man, crimson with rage, turned to his nephew: 'You hear him. He calls me coward and in my own house. Throw the beggar out.' He turned back to Alasdair. 'We should have driven you and your family out of this Glen fifty years ago,' he raged.

He stopped his ravings to gasp for breath. Somewhat recovered, he focused his attention on Jamie once more. 'I ordered you to throw this man out of our house.' He spoke quietly now, low and menacing.

'ARE YOU DEAF!' The scream echoed in the hall.

Jamie blanched, but stared unblinkingly at his uncle.

'I am deaf to such an order. Alasdair is right. We ran at Culloden, true enough, but not out of cowardice. A Highlander is a brave warrior, but a canny one. He knows full well when a cause is lost. He does not mind running when that is all there is left for him to do. And now we are rats caught in a trap of our own making, and there is no choice left to us. It is only a matter of time before the English come. I shall not wait here to be cut down in my own home. I shall fight them where and when I decree.'

The giant turned quickly on his heels and marched from the room, leaving his astonished uncle and an even more astonished Alasdair staring after him. Alasdair had not dared hope for such support, and old McIan had never heard his nephew deliver such an eloquent or lengthy speech before. The old man turned to Alasdair, his eyes still retaining some of their fury.

'Take what arms and provisions you might need for your journey. I give you no men.' Before Alasdair could respond, the Chief had stomped to the door, but stopped at the last moment. 'Your wife and the other women of your family may stay here while you are gone. Good luck, you impudent puppy. May Fingal's blood flow in your veins. You will need it.'

When the old man had gone, Alasdair felt a rush of excitement course through his body. He knew all at once that the spirit of the clans had not died, no matter how much their numbers were depleted.

He raced to Jamie's room. The big man let out a roar of joy to hear the news and went off to select horses and provisions for their journey. 'We ride after dawn tomorrow,' he shouted behind him as he pounded down the corridor. Alasdair went to his wife's room. Kathy sat by the window, humming as she watched the sun's rays disappear over Loch Leven, and did not notice her husband's presence until he gently touched her shoulder. Her startled look turned to one of pleasure as she gazed up at him.

For a moment his rash scheme hung in the balance as he searched her beautiful, trusting, expectant face. How could he leave her now that she needed him so badly, he wondered, and, as he had to admit to himself, he needed her.

Silently she rose and kissed him, tenderly at first and then with a breathless insistency that excited him. Her lips grew hot under his and his hands began to explore her full body. Suddenly, he was tearing at her garments, short, sharp snorts of air escaping from their nostrils. They made love passionately as Alasdair attempted to force the memory of the hated Englishman from her mind. When they had finished they lay for a while, breathing gently in the plain dark-wooded room, locked in each other's arms.

He propped himself on his elbow and drew her head to his breast so that he would not have to look at her.

'Dear Kathy,' he haltingly began, 'I do not know how to tell you this, but I . . . ' he faltered, his courage failing him for once.

'You must leave me.' She spoke the words in a tone of quiet finality.

'You know!' He was genuinely astonished.

'Yes. I do not want to lose you again so soon, but I know you will not rest until you feel your duty is done. I am your wife. I understand.'

For the first time since the morning overlooking the village from the escarpment, Alasdair burst into tears and cried far into the night until sleep came to restore his mind and body for the ordeal ahead – an ordeal the scope and length of which he could not have imagined.

In the early morning, he rose and kissed his sleeping wife. He dressed by the light which came faintly through the window, and as he donned his plaid, hose, jacket, bonnet, shoes and claymore, he stared up the Glen. A lone moorcock wheeled in the air, wings gently stroking the wind currents that sustained its flight. The early morning sun was golden and a stillness, a feeling of supreme peace covered the valley like soft heather. Alasdair watched and allowed himself to share in that sensation of contentment for a moment. It would be some time he knew before he would experience it again.

He turned from the window and studied his wife. 'I will be back soon and we will escape to France,' he whispered before leaving the room. He did not have the courage to waken her.

Below he joined Jamie in a swift breakfast of curds and bread. Without a word they finished their food and strode out of the house to their horses.

Their steeds were waiting for them, sturdy animals but light enough to gallop like the wind when necessary. Jamie had chosen well.

Jamie turned to Alasdair.

'After they left your village the soldiers turned into Rannoch. As they passed this way to your place, they must have come from Fort William. I am sure they will return there. We might be too late to catch them, but we can try.'

Alasdair bared his teeth in a frightening grimace.

'We will follow their path. We have debts to collect.' The hairs on Jamie's neck bristled at the sound of his companion's voice. There was a trace of evil in it.

They leapt on their horses, and soon the sound of thundering hooves rent the peace of an early summer morning in Glencoe.

There were debts to be collected.

CHAPTER THREE

THE CAPTAIN

At night a grim blackness descends on Rannoch Moor, broken
only by the piercing pinpoints of light provided by the stars
that overlook that cold, desolate place. Winds howl continuously across the peat-filled wastes, and the sound takes on a
fearful, inhuman quality in the accompanying darkness, as if
the warriors of Celtic legend had returned under its cover to
bemoan their collective fate.

On the night following the start of Alasdair MacDonald
and Jamie McIan's quest, an extra light flickered eerily across
the moor and strange, carefree noises mingled with the sound
of the wind.

Captain Hinchcliffe was drunk and so were his men.

After the pillage of Alasdair MacDonald's village, they had
turned into Rannoch, where they had been ordered to stay
for one week.

'Take a dozen soldiers on foot to Glencoe and check to see
how many of those rascally MacDonalds have returned from
Culloden. Ascertain numbers and general condition, but do not
come into contact with them unless you are left with no
choice. Do you understand?' His commanding officer had
already assessed his new Captain's character and was determined not to give ambiguous orders. 'And when you've done
that, proceed to Rannoch. Stay there for a week and ascertain how many rebels return by that route. Again, do not
attack. This is an intelligence mission, not a punitive one. And
remember, Captain, you cannot afford to fail after your recent
conduct. You are dismissed.'

Hinchcliffe had cursed this turn of events at first. One Campbell scout could have done the job as easily, but then he had
realised his extraordinary luck. An ideal opportunity for
revenge had just presented itself. Glencoe was the home of
that damn Alasdair MacDonald. He would use his mission to
repay the scoundrel for his actions at Culloden.

His revenge had been sweet, but by no means complete. MacDonald's family had been a simple target, and he had certainly enjoyed taking that black-haired beauty. Perhaps she had been MacDonald's wife. The irony would have been too delicious. He shivered, half in memory of her body, half in imagining Alasdair MacDonald's homecoming. The brave hero, the Highland warrior with no one to greet him or sing his praises. Hinchcliffe laughed out loud, a sneering guffaw that his men had rapidly learnt to hate.

Still, his chance for complete revenge had not gone. There was always a chance that MacDonald would return by way of Rannoch. They had already spotted a large group of returning natives of Glencoe, but the force had been too large to attack and Alasdair had not been among them. If it had been Alasdair who had escaped them through the passage in the mountain there was a good chance that he might follow, hoping for revenge. Hinchcliffe would be ready for him.

His men had used the time on Rannoch wisely. They had ferreted out the broken men of the Moor, those Highlanders cast out from their own clans who eked a miserable existence out of the unyielding landscape.

On that very evening the troops had discovered a cache of whisky hidden in the crude thatching of one of the broken men's miserable hovels. Nine good bottles between thirteen men. All of them were royally drunk. As the hour of two in the morning approached and passed, the men began dozing, but Hinchcliffe, sitting apart from them, stayed awake, mulling over the events that had led him to this God-forsaken place. He was alone with only twelve ruffians and a horse for company in the middle of a deserted moor, with no protection from the howling wind and sleeting rain that continually made life so miserable.

This was no place, he decided, for a civilised soldier. Certainly no place for Captain Forbes Hinchcliffe, more used as he was to the gaming clubs and brothels of London. Most evenings would have found him dressed in the height of fashion, complete with powdered wig and artfully placed mole, taking his pleasure in whoring, gambling and drinking. Not, he admitted, far removed from the favoured pastimes of most of the men under his command, but he at least indulged himself with civilised people in civilised society. What would have been designated brutal savagery in a redcoat appeared more as high spirits in a member of Hinchcliffe's class. Not that Hinch-

31

cliffe's behaviour gained the general approbation of his elders. Far from it. His father had been forced to find him some occupation to curb the worst of his son's excesses. He had not chosen wisely. He had had no better luck with his cavalry regiments than with the educational establishments he had graced. A promising career at Eton had been spoilt by a surfeit of sodomy and drink in his last year. He took the practices with him to King's College at Cambridge, the traditional home of Eton's graduates, where he discovered the delights of the female form and the deep pleasure to be gained from spending his father's money in gambling. A vicious fight in one of the town's most notorious ale houses had ended in the death of three townsfolk and Hinchcliffe's sending down. With a great deal of expenditure, his father had arranged for his entry into one of the most fashionable Cavalry regiments, but Hinchcliffe had not taken kindly to the discipline. The next few years were spent in moving from one regiment to another. He would have been court-martialled on several occasions had his father, one of England's most eminent lawyers, not been a great personal friend of the King.

By the time that Prince Charles Edward Stuart had landed in Scotland, Hinchcliffe had once more been in a most pleasurable state of limbo in the capital. That unfortunately had been well and truly shattered by the arrival of the Young Pretender claiming the throne of England for his papist father. In the desperate panic following the gathering of the clans under Charles's banner, Hinchcliffe had been given a posting as a captain in Kingston's Horse. By a series of elaborate subterfuges, he had been able to delay the appointment until the young prince and his rebels had been safely beaten back over the border of Scotland. Circumstances had finally conjoined, however, to make the Captain's escape from London imperative. A lady of his acquaintance, Arabella Fitzmorton, had found herself to be with child, which would not have given her husband undue cause for alarm had it not been for the fact that, being ill with the pox, he had not slept with her for nearly two years.

A savage beating on the door of his Albany flat, accompanied by loud and terrible threats from Mr Fitzmorton had convinced Hinchcliffe that his duty lay with his regiment.

Two months later he had found himself drawn up with Kingston's Horse at Culloden. His return to active duty had not been quick enough for his commanding officer, and he now found himself riding with a volunteer regiment made up of tradesmen and apprentices from Nottinghamshire, but despite his personal embarrassment he had laughed loud and long at the sight of the crazed Highlanders falling like flies under the onslaught of English grapeshot, and had been the first through the line of Poultney's Rifles when ordered to attack the fleeing rebels. Then he had become bored with the admittedly fairly amusing task of cutting down defenceless men from the safety of his horse. As his own fellow troops caught up with him, he wheeled his horse around and returned to where the richest-looking Highlanders had fallen, close to the original British line.

Shooing away some of the footsoldiers who had already begun the task of relieving the dead and dying of valuable possessions, he ran quickly from body to body removing anything that looked remotely saleable. His father had refused to pay any more of his gambling debts, and there were many awkward ones outstanding back in London.

The fifth or sixth corpse he had searched looked particularly promising. A handsome ring glinted from one of its fingers. A ruby, if the Captain wasn't mistaken. He eagerly ripped it off the finger and began an examination of the jacket pockets. He let out a scream of terror as two hands reached for his throat and engaged him in a vice-like grip. The Highlander, whom Hinchcliffe had supposed dead, rose to his knees whilst keeping his grip, and stared into the Captain's eyes with such fury that Hinchcliffe chilled to the very centre of his being. Gripping the throat with one hand, the Highlander drew back the other hand and crashed his fist into the side of the Captain's mouth.

The Captain fell to the ground, the sweet taste of blood filling his mouth. Three of his teeth had been broken.

He watched dimly as the Highlander – even in his own misery Hinchcliffe could see that the man was severely wounded in the side – staggered to his feet and mounted the Captain's horse. The Highlander turned in the saddle and smiled an infuriatingly insulting smile at the prone officer before galloping off in the direction of his MacDonald colleagues.

As Hinchcliffe lay on the ground, coughing blood and desperately trying to regain his breath, he heard the sound of laughter. A soft, melodious, deeply-mocking laugh that grated on his already badly-shaken nerves. He struggled to regain an upright posture and found himself surrounded by redcoats, some of whom were openly chortling at him. They avoided his eyes as he stared at each man in turn, but nothing could abate their amusement.

Near to the Captain lay a wounded Highlander. One of his legs had been severed at the knee. The lower half of his leg lay about a yard away from him, oddly pathetic in its incompleteness. He was the source of the laugh.

Tears of humiliation and anger sprang to the Captain's eyes. He lurched towards the Highlander and stood over him, shaking with rage. The Highlander paused and licked his dry lips. 'Well, my fine Englishman, you tangled with young Alasdair MacDonald of Glencoe, and he made a proper fool of you. I'll die happy for seeing such a glorious sight.' He stopped for a moment, unable to contain himself, and began laughing again before resuming. 'God, you must be a very stupid man, for all your gold braid.'

Hinchcliffe ripped his dagger from his belt and fell on the man in a frenzy, hacking at his flesh, tearing his jacket, ripping his cheeks open. The Highlander's throat expelled a strange rattling sound as the hysterical knife found his heart, severing the main pulmonary artery.

And so Simon Gregor became the first wounded man to be needlessly slaughtered after the battle of Culloden. Hundreds were to suffer his fate as the British troops began an orgy of slaughter and sadism on a moor that would give its name to the most infamous military encounter in British history.

During that day, and the next, blood ran freely as Englishmen and Lowland Scots alike laughed crazily as they marched from one wounded man to the next, severing heads, torturing with bayonets, castrating still-conscious men, their uniforms stained all over with a deeper and more shameful red than that of their coats.

During that night Hinchcliffe's name became an excuse to laugh even louder. Every soldier knew the story and would not tire of repeating it. His misery lessened somewhat the next day when his commanding officer called him to his tent.

The man sat sipping Madeira, but offered none to his Captain. 'Kingston's Horse are going to Inverness to prepare a reception for rebel prisoners. You, sir, shall go to Fort William in the west to gather information so that we might plan our activities in that region over the coming months. You have proved yourself to be a greedy, incompetent buffoon. Mr Fitzmorton, whose wife you have shamed, is a friend of mine. It gives me the greatest pleasure to dismiss you from this

34

regiment. I shall not order a formal court-martial. You will merely transfer' – the word became a long, yawning sneer – 'to different duties. Try, for the sake of your poor father, to regain some honour by doing a good and decent job. I fear, however, that it will prove quite beyond you.' He paused, picked up a quill and began signing documents. 'You're a bloody scoundrel. Get out of my sight.' He stabbed the pen into an ink well.

Hinchcliffe felt relief as he slunk from the tent and made his way to his own quarters, his eyes cast to the ground lest he catch the smirks that would have been his daily lot had he remained in camp with his own regiment. He would soon put a stop to any of that nonsense with the men who would accompany him to Fort William.

One name kept coming to his mind as he prepared for his journey, and it remained with him during the few days it took to reach his new post. He could still see the Highlander on his horse, staring down at him, a look of utter contempt on his face. Hinchcliffe would know what to do with that face if ever a chance presented itself.

His men were snoring loudly now, and as the fire burned itself out, the Captain's eyes began to close. There was something intangible, however, that kept him from falling into the welcoming arms of sleep.

A tremor of fear passed over the Captain's body.

CHAPTER FOUR

THE CLAN

Alasdair and Jamie noted the Captain's drooping eyelids. Alasdair's mouth twisted into the grimace that had frightened Jamie back in Invercoe.

'How shall we attack, Alasdair?' McIan whispered hoarsely, his voice betraying his eagerness.

'We shall rush them. I shall be quite happy if we only accomplish the death of that damn man in the blue coat.'

'Aye, well and good, my friend, but I would not mind walking away from this encounter.' Jamie sounded faintly worried.

'Very well, McIan, I forgot myself. There is a possibility that we might kill him without disturbing the others. They are very drunk. I shall creep up to him, slit his throat as they slit my son's and melt into the night. We will be gone before the rest have awoken.'

Jamie interrupted – 'I shall do it. I am good with a knife.'

'Aye, and you are twice my size and twice the target. Don't talk daft, man. This is my business and I am well equipped for it.'

They crept forward on their bellies, pain shooting through Alasdair's side as his wound rubbed against the ground. As they approached to within fifteen yards of the Captain Alasdair reached out his hand to signal for Jamie to stop. If anything should happen to Alasdair, Jamie would at least have a chance of reaching the horses standing some sixty yards away.

Alasdair, crept forward, hand on dirk, his face red in the glowing embers of the dying fire. His eyes glittered and he was breathing in short gasps.

He was five yards from his prey, when with startling speed, the Captain leapt to his feet, his pistol aimed straight at Alasdair's head.

'Good evening, Mr MacDonald, or should I say good morning. I somehow knew that we should meet again. I am so pleased.'

36

Alasdair recognised him now. The man who had stolen his ruby ring and provided his means of escape from the battle-field. As he lay there, a chill of fear gripped his stomach. Hinchcliffe's men started waking up, shaking their drink-befuddled heads in an attempt to absorb the extraordinary scene before them.

Hinchcliffe motioned two of his men to step forward and pick up Alasdair.

As they moved towards him, two things happened.

Alasdair rolled over on to his side so that the oncoming soldiers acted as a shield between him and the Captain's gun, and out of the shadows sprang the huge figure of Jamie McIan accompanied by a blood-curdling yell and the swooping noise of a claymore slicing through the air.

The soldier standing behind Hinchcliffe hardly saw the fear-some warrior before he died, his head split neatly between his two bloodshot eyes. Jamie, abandoning the sword which lay wedged between the dead man's shoulder blades, drew his dirk and leapt at Hinchcliffe. The astonished Captain involun-tarily squeezed the trigger of his pistol, which was aiming at the ground. The noise and smoke of the retort confused Jamie, who found himself grasping at the air. Hinchcliffe, brought to his senses by the explosion, had neatly side-stepped the large man, and now stood, a second pistol in his hand aimed at Jamie's mystified head.

Alasdair had fared little better. One of the advancing soldiers had received a slight dirk wound in his leg, but Alas-dair soon found himself with four bayonets pointed at his neck and four angry pairs of eyes staring down rifle barrels at him.

Everything was still for a moment. The Highlanders tensed themselves for the death they had surely earned. The soldiers stood like wax figures in the dim light of the dying fire.

Hinchcliffe pulled himself together. He had been standing, pistol aimed at the burly ruffian's skull, wondering what to do with the two rebels, or to be precise, exactly how he was going to kill them. He dismissed the big man. Straight shooting for him, as there was no tree nearby to give him a proper rebel's execution.

Alasdair's was a difficult case, however. He deserved some-thing out of the ordinary. Hinchcliffe smiled. Of course.

'That one over there, bring him near the fire. Stake out his arms and legs. Spreadeagle him. We'll provide our guests with some entertainment before the night is out. Get the fire going again and take this big ox over there so that he may watch his companion's fate.'

The men scurried about their work, fetching ropes, putting small stakes in the ground, their heads cleared by the rudeness of their awakening.

Jamie's large hands were tied behind his back, the rope being brought down to encompass his ankles. He lay, sobbing with frustration, his legs drawn up behind him till they touched his hands, and watched the strange preparations going on around Alasdair.

The pegs in the ground formed a perfect square. Alasdair's hands and feet were attached by rope to each of the pegs. His legs and arms were twisted in opposite directions until they were almost at right angles to the body. When he struggled, one of the soldiers placed his knee firmly into his wounded side. He yelled and slumped back, nearly resigned to his fate.

Hinchcliffe knelt by the fire, adding peat and wood until the flames flared up once more. He walked to his horse and retrieved a large knife with an ornate, jewelled handle and nine-inch blade from his saddlebag. He walked back to the fire and plunged the knife up to the hilt in the flames. He let go of the handle and it stuck obscenely upwards, held in place by two parallel logs. He walked to Alasdair's side. The Highlander refused to meet his gaze.

'So you will not look upon me, Mr MacDonald? That was not the case last week when you stole my horse. Well, I will now endeavour to make sure that you never look upon anyone again.' He guffawed, throwing his head back. The sound echoed hollowly in the night. He returned his attention to his secured victim.

'Your family was well, I trust, on your return? I was fortunate enough to meet them two days ago. They did not seem pleased to see me. I cannot think why.' His voice was a nasal sing-song. 'But I believe I was able to give one of them great pleasure. A pretty, black-haired lass with whom I had occasion to lie seemed delighted with my endeavours. A relative, perhaps?'

Alasdair could control himself no longer. His vain resolve not to give the monster pleasure by showing his feelings evaporated in a stream of violent abuse.

The Captain continued against the volley of Gaelic and

English. 'So it was your wife. I am so glad I was able to afford her some pleasure.'

Alasdair screamed: 'You bastard, you filthy, heathen son of a dog!' His body arched into the air, his arms and legs threshing in an attempt to escape the ropes.

Hinchcliffe kicked him expertly in the side where his old wound had started once more to ooze blood. Alasdair shrieked at the pain.

Hinchcliffe was no longer smiling. He spoke quickly, a hint of madness in his voice. 'Yes, MacDonald, I killed your family and I had your wife, but the enormous pleasure that gave me is nothing to the pleasure I now feel. I am about to demonstrate a rather witty trick devised by the Indians of North America. My brother has just written to me from that place and described how the redskinned natives take their revenge upon their enemies.'

He paused, breathing harshly through his nose.

'He was reliably informed that they use a heated knife to remove their victim's scalp and tongue. They then blind him and turn him loose. He lives, apparently, for several hours in the most excruciating pain. I replied to my brother's correspondence complaining that England offered few opportunities for such experiments. And now you have proved me quite wrong. You have made a fool of me again. It will be the last time.'

Alasdair's struggle had become so violent during the Captain's horrifying speech that two soldiers were forced to restrain him lest he break his bonds. As he became subdued he caught one of the soldier's eyes. He was a young boy, probably no more than sixteen and his face still bore the marks of the beating Hinchcliffe had inflicted on him. His eyes were wide in terror, and as they met Alasdair's, there seemed a trace of compassion in them, as if he were as frightened by Hinchcliffe's intentions as Alasdair himself.

When Alasdair had become quite still, they rose. Alasdair cleared his throat. 'Sir, as you know, I am a Catholic. I should like the opportunity to confess before I die. At the very least let me loose so that I may make my prayers in an attitude of fiitting devotion.'

Hinchcliffe snorted in derision. 'Yes, Mr MacDonald, I know the creed you follow. Permission denied. It will add piquancy to the situation to know that you will meet your maker unshriven. Imagine it. A revenge reaching into the afterlife. Say your prayers where you lie. You had better say them quickly, for I am anxious to begin my experiment.'

He turned away from Alasdair, who closed his eyes and made peace with his God as well as circumstances would allow, and walked to the fire. The Englishman wrapped a lace handkerchief several times around his hand before stooping to pick up the knife which glowed white against the night sky. He examined the blade fondly, twirling it back and forth, its glow illuminating his handsome face.

The soldiers stood around the fire looking apprehensively at their commander. One or two found it difficult to believe that he meant to carry out his threats, but most were resigned to it. Brutality was regarded as normal behaviour by troops used to receiving 300 lashes for selling their bread ration.

As the Captain walked back to Alasdair, most of the men stepped forward in order to obtain a better view.

The Captain beckoned two of them to restrain Alasdair's limbs.

As Hinchcliffe bent down, Jamie, lying some ten paces away, let out a howl of protest, his eyes bulging in disbelief. The Captain walked over to him, holding the still glowing knife in front.

'Do not worry, my large friend. I have decided in view of your outbursts to let you enjoy the same fate, but not until you have enjoyed our little play. In the meantime you will have to be content with a small taste of what is to come.' He leant forward and pressed the flat blade of the knife against an exposed part of McIan's thigh. There was a sizzling sound. Smoke curled upwards. McIan's piercing scream carried clear across Rannoch.

'Satisfied?' Hinchcliffe asked as he turned away. McIan's skin bore an angry red welt where the blade had pressed into it.

Hinchcliffe strolled back to Alasdair, bent down and grabbed his hair.

'Now, let us undo some of Nature's fine work.'

As the knife travelled towards Alasdair's head, its journey was interrupted by a loud cry.

By the fire, the young soldier who had been forced to restrain Alasdair had fallen to his knees and was wringing his hands. 'Captain, in God's name please spare the man. In the name of our Church you cannot do this,' he spluttered between sobs. Hinchcliffe jumped to his feet.

'You tell me I cannot do this?' he cried. 'I can do as I damn well please. Bring the boy here. I will educate him.'

Two of the soldiers detached themselves from the group gathered near the body and dragged the crying boy to where Alasdair lay.

'Hold his head down there where he can get a better view of the proceedings. Do not try to look away, boy, or you will suffer the same fate. Do you understand?'

The youth's head nodded in miserable acquiescence.

'Good, then we can continue.'

The knife skirted up Alasdair's right cheek, scorching his beard. He could feel the heat approaching his eyes. He resumed his prayers and squeezed his eyes tight shut, tensing his body against the appalling pain that was soon to come.

Then, as the blade prodded into the closed eyelids, there was the sound of a soft thud and the trooper next to Hinchcliffe gave a big sigh before falling across Alasdair's body. He was dead, a knife sticking far into his back.

The troops drew their swords and pistols. Strange howling noises assailed them from all sides, seemingly from just beyond the dim light of the fire. A cry came from the direction of McIan's body. They all turned. There was no sign of the soldier who had been guarding him. From the shadows strode McIan, ropes dangling from his wrists, a claymore in his hand and a terrible expression on his face. The troops bolted in all directions, convinced that scores of murderous Highlanders lay waiting to attack. Two soldiers blundered near McIan. Two deft strokes cut them down. Three more redcoats met their death just beyond the glow of the fire, their screams lost in the confused, terrified yowlings of their running companions.

Hinchcliffe had been the first to bolt. He had raced towards the fire, cleared it in a leap, and had taken off in the direction of his horse.

All was silent, save for one whimpering soldier slumped on the ground a few yards from the fire. It was the redcoat who had slit the child's belly in Alasdair's village. The fright had been too much for him and he had evacuated his bowels.

From the shadows strode two men, kilted, wild-haired, their claymores pointing directly in front. They were unsmiling as they stood looking down at Alasdair whose bonds were being cut by McIan.

As Alasdair sat up, rubbing his wrists and ankles where the

41

ropes had cut through his skin, he looked at McIan and they both slowly turned their heads to face the newcomers.

McIan spoke. 'We cannot thank you enough for what you have done. I felt sure that all was lost when you appeared to cut my ropes. With all that noise you made, they must have thought a hundred of us had turned up.'

He laughed excitedly, but the men remained silent.

Alasdair got up unsteadily. His blood had not yet begun to circulate properly. 'We owe you a great debt.' Again there was silence.

'Will you not speak to us?'

McIan interrupted. 'I think I know why you do not speak. You are broken men. You have been cast out from your clan. Am I right?'

The men looked at each other.

At length, and with apparent effort, one of them spoke.

'You are right. We are the banished ones. You must know that my very act of speaking to you is punishable by my death.'

The two strangers turned to leave.

Alasdair limped over to them and turned the first one round to face him. He placed his hands on his shoulders and kissed him once on each cheek. 'Whatever you have done in the past, you have acted tonight as noble Highlanders. Prince Charlie himself would have been proud of you.'

They stood, tendrils of wild, greasy hair snaking in the wind. Their faces were still expressionless, but tears had sprung to their eyes. They seemed uncertain of what to do.

Alasdair tried again. 'We know that your crime must have been great for such a fate to befall you, but it is now time to forget the past. It lies dead at Culloden' – he unconsciously echoed the words of his Chief – 'We are all broken men. The English have slaughtered the clans at Culloden Moor.'

The men gasped.

'Did you not know?' asked McIan, astonished.

'We had no idea. We knew that something important was happening. For the past two weeks clansmen and redcoats have been crossing the Moor. We have been in hiding, for people have been coming by our hut where normally no one travels. But the clans defeated? And is Prince Charlie still in the country?'

McIan assured them that the Prince had escaped.

'Is that why you are in such a terrible state, because you have been in hiding?' asked Alasdair.

'No. When you do not deal with society, there seems little point in keeping up appearances. We are not considered human, so we do not generally act as such.'

'Well, you are more than human to us,' Alasdair assured them. 'We intend to pay back the English for their crimes. Will you help us?'

Alasdair looked at them, his eyes pleading his cause. 'Sir, you pay us an honour far greater than you can realise. You should not be speaking to us, let alone offering companionship. If you are serious, and are prepared to suffer the consequences, we will join you.'

The man stepped forward and offered his hand.

'I am Hugh Gregor. My quiet friend is Lindsay Hamish, another member of Clan Gregor, and a close companion for many years.'

Jamie and Alasdair introduced themselves.

'Well, by God, we look a devilish team,' Jamie laughingly remarked.

Alasdair turned to him slowly.

'As we are from separate clans, and our new companions are not officially members of any clan, perhaps we should form our own. A clan dedicated to continuing the fight against the English, not for Prince Charles, or for Catholicism, but for ourselves, the Highlanders who own and rule this land.' He stared in front, an idea forming in his mind. 'As the English would rather meet the Devil himself than meet with us, from this day we shall be the Devil's Clan.'

The spines of the four men tingled, and an electric atmosphere charged the air around them. Their hands moved forward automatically to a point where they all met. In unison they chanted: 'The Devil's Clan.'

CHAPTER FIVE

THE WELCOME

The four men stood by the flickering light of the fire, their rough tartan kilts furling against their legs in the billowing wind that whipped Rannoch Moor. A moan broke the silence. It came from the lips of the terrified redcoat who had failed to escape. He was about forty years of age, an ugly man with a bulbous nose disfigured by the tackets common to the habitual drinker. His eyes still bulged with fear and tears had left clean tracks through the dirt on his cheeks. That part of his face not covered with unkempt stubble was laced with small scars, the reminders of some childhood disease.

The man was, not a coward. He had often stood in line against fearsome opposition while his comrades had been butchered on either side of him. The thought of bolting for safety or of giving up the fight to beg for mercy had never crossed his mind. As a soldier, he had simply been taught the correctness of certain procedures, and as long as he was not asked to make decisions as to his own actions, he followed those procedures to the letter. But this, this was different. Wild animals hurtling at him from the darkness, with strange cries and contorted faces, their swords glinting in the firelight. This was not proper soldiering, and these were not proper soldiers. More like demons out of hell. None of this had been included in his training, or anything like it in twenty years of practical experience fighting for King and Country.

As the four Highlanders walked towards the terrified soldier, he glanced nervously at each of them in turn. Their eyes were hard on him, but the close presence of his enemies was oddly reassuring and he felt his fear die slowly away.

Alasdair spoke. 'What is your name?'

'Jackson. Thomas Jackson.' He spoke with a strong Cornish accent.

'Why did you destroy my village, Jackson?'

'Orders.' The soldier nodded his head to stress the point.

44

'Whose orders, Jackson?' Alasdair's voice was tight, controlled.

'Why, the Captain's, sir. Captain Hinchcliffe.'

'Do you always obey orders, Jackson?'

'Why yes, sir. No point in being a soldier lessen you obey orders,' he replied without hesitation.

'Even when they demand you kill a child?' Alasdair's voice was bitter. A look of fear flitted across the man's face. He quickly recomposed his features, but it was too late. Alasdair had noted his deepening guilt.

'Did you enjoy skewering the child, my brave warrior? Is that what they teach you in the King's Army? When you face grown men, it appears you cannot even control your bowels.' The Highlanders snorted with contemptuous laughter and the soldier's face turned crimson with shame despite the coldness of the night.

The man spoke hurriedly. 'I was obeying orders. How I killed the child is not important. Anyway, 'tis but your own fault. I have no learning and even I can see that truth. You have tried to overthrow the King. You are rebels and have placed yourselves outside the law. How do you expect to be treated?'

'Like men! Like soldiers. Look at me.' Alasdair bent down towards the man. 'Am I so different from you?' Jackson stared into Alasdair's eyes for a moment and tried to get up, but Hugh Gregor pushed him back with his foot.

Frustrated, he began to talk again. 'Why should we treat you any different. We've been told about you, how you live. Like animals. That's all you are. Animals!' His voice had risen to a shriek.

Hugh Gregor stepped forward. 'No man speaks like that about my people.' He raised his sword above his head with both hands and stood, poised, ready to break the soldier's skull. Suddenly Alasdair launched himself at Hugh, catching him with his head full in his stomach. Hugh buckled over and lay on the ground gasping for air. Alasdair bent to help him but was angrily shrugged away.

'Come, come.' Jamie bent forward and levered Hugh roughly to his feet. 'This is no way for companions to behave towards each other. Think of the oath we have just sworn.' Hugh coughed as air re-entered his lungs and nodded his head in quiet assent.

Alasdair turned to face the soldier once more.

'True, we do not always behave as gentlemen, but the stories you have been told about us are no doubt greatly exaggerated. We are a warrior people forced to carve a living out of the sparse soil of these lands. We are quick to anger and slow to form friendships, except . . . ' he paused and turned to smile at Hugh Gregor and Lindsay Hamish ' . . . for tonight, perhaps. We have too much pride and too much skill with our weapons to live peaceable lives. Insults must be avenged and our justice is rough and maybe barbaric – although I would have thought the word had little meaning for such as yourself – but it is justice nevertheless.'

He half-turned away from the bewildered soldier and stared into the night across the moor. The silence was broken by the cry of a lone bird.

'We do not ask that you understand our life. Only that you leave us in peace to live it as we think fit. The MacDonalds were once the Lords of the Isles and held dominion over the Western Isles and this dourful coast. Centuries of fierce fighting won this land for us, and all we asked was the right to rule it, but the Lowlanders came, then the English, with their petty laws born out of soft living and fertile land, and they bound us tight with their laws and divided our people even further. Some, like the damned Campbells,' his face contorted with deep contempt, 'supported these enemies and have won their battles for them.'

Alasdair sighed and turned back to the soldier.

'When Charles came we were bound to follow him. He has promised us back our lands. I have no wish to rule your country. A pox on it. But conquering you and your masters was our only hope of living here on our own terms. This is our land, redcoat. How can a man be a traitor who fights for the right to govern his own land? It is the Campbells who are the traitors.' He broke off suddenly to stare at the prostrate soldier. 'You poor fool. You haven't understood a word, have you?'

Jamie, obviously affected by a speech in which he could recognise his own beliefs given voice, walked slowly over to Alasdair and patted him on the back. Hugh Gregor, who had stared at the ground throughout the speech, some resentment at being denied the death of the soldier still smouldering within him, turned to face his new-found companion, and grinned.

'After such a speech, man, I'll forgive you everything.' Lindsay Hamish nodded his head in agreement.

46

'Thank you my friends.' Alasdair dipped into his jacket pocket and produced a silver crucifix about four inches in length. He dangled it by its chain in front of the soldier.

'You are not a quick-witted man, but I think you will recognise this.'

'Of course I does,' the man answered, obvious confusion in his tone. Alasdair's speech had indeed made little sense to him, and he had spent most of the time in preparing himself for death.

'Good,' Alasdair walked to fire and lowered the cross into the embers. As he crouched on his haunches, he spoke.

'I shall not kill you, although you do not deserve to live. Instead I will brand you with the symbol of my religion. You will wear the mark of the cross as a warning to others.' He lifted the crucifix out of the fire. It glowed brightly, as Hinchcliffe's knife had done minutes before.

'Hold him still,' he rasped, and his companions, uncertain themselves as to his plan, fell on the soldier, lying across his limbs to prevent him moving. Alasdair dangled the cross in front of the man's eyes, the soldier's neck craned and the veins on his temple bulged obscenely. Alasdair gripped him savagely by his hair and rammed the cross against his forehead. There was a smell of burning flesh and the man screamed in pain. The Highlanders released his limbs and as he clutched feebly at the ugly red wound he moaned softly.

Alasdair rubbed the still-hot metal against the cold earth and put it back in his pocket. He would have need of it again.

He stood and looked at the soldier, his eyes cold in the aftermath of revenge, while his companions fetched their horses from the surrounding darkness.

'Where to?' asked Jamie when they had returned.

'I don't know,' answered Alasdair. 'We must plan our next move carefully . . . after we have all had some rest.' Hugh Gregor spoke hesitantly. 'I have not seen my family for many months. When we came to Rannoch, I left my wife to live with my sister. I did not want her to share this.' He gestured vaguely about him. 'I do not know how the village will treat us. I do not even know how my wife will react to my return.'

Alasdair smiled. 'As a wife. She will forgive you. Our women get used to it, for we all do many things that require forgiveness.'

Hugh thought for a moment.

'What I have done is difficult to forgive.'

'One day you might tell us. Until then, lead away. I'm much in need of sleep.' Alasdair turned to face the redcoat who had stumbled to his feet and now stood staring at them, dabbing mud on his forehead to deaden the pain.

Alasdair shouted to him. 'Tell your brave companions that they will not sleep easy while we roam this country. Tell them that, friend, and you will have earned your reprieve.'

The horses reared and wheeled, and the four riders plunged into the darkness. The soldier buried his face in his hands and slumped to the ground, sobbing with relief. Against all the odds, Thomas Jackson's life had been spared.

The windows of the house had completely steamed over. An outsider looking in would have dimly made out swirling forms in rapid movement. Inside, bodies danced and pranced and intermingled, and sweat-stained faces glistening demoniacally in the light of a roaring fire as people jigged and reeled and wheeled, arms locked, now loose, now falling over, now leaping in the air. The pipes whined and churned with ever-increasing speed and in ever-stranger swirls of crazy tunes, and the bodhráns clattered and battered insanely reaching beyond each new crescendo of noise until the people felt they could stand it no longer.

The sparsely-furnished room contained two long plain wood tables that creaked under the weight of pots of stew and strong-smelling broth, and bottles of fine French claret and kegs of powerful brandy surrounded by wooden drinking vessels and delicately-patterned Jacobite glasses. For relief there were mounds of barley-cakes and a plentiful supply of whisky sweetened with honey.

Over thirty people were crowded into the small room, women, children and old men. Most were deliriously happy, some were near to dropping with exhaustion brought on by a surfeit of heat and dancing, and some had already fallen to the floor.

The Gregors had come to welcome their lost sheep, and had not been slow to accept their new-found friends. With unusual delicacy, no one had mentioned the cause of their banishment, or the event itself, and everyone had produced their last supplies of good drink to mark the occasion. There had been little chance for celebration of late. The few men who had returned from Culloden had continued their journey

48

after a few hours, convinced that the soldiers were on their tail and that their families would be safer without their presence. Now the villagers' weeks of uncertainty and fear had erupted in a glorious party. There was more than a hint of desperation in their merry-making, for few believed that they would ever see their menfolk again. Even the return of Hugh and Lindsay, two men banished in shame, had been some recompense for their misery.

Every now and then the white-bearded musicians would allow the revellers a chance to regain breath by playing dirges and laments. Mostly they played those songs traditionally associated with the Gregor clan, but included the occasional MacDonald lament when Jamie McIan's drunken urgings threatened to spill into violence. The Gregors and the Mac-Donalds, although usually teamed together against their common enemy, the Campbells, did not always live in harmony. Jamie was on the verge of giving a practical demonstration of this division when a familiar, haunting melody served to cool his drink-inflamed temper. As he stood at least a head above all others in the room, no one felt inclined to argue with him.

'Play away, my brave boys. Now there's a tune a man could weep at.' So saying, large, sentimental tears began to course down his cheeks as he hummed along with the pipes, destroying the melody for all those listening

Alasdair sat in a corner, refusing to join in the celebrations. Only once did he consent to dance, and then only when his host threatened to lose patience with him. He danced for a short while with Hugh Gregor's wife, Eileen, and noted with a pang of regret the joy that shone in her eyes. It only made what he had to do so much more difficult.

Hugh Gregor and Lindsay Hamish led the festivities with gusto, delighted at being reunited with their families. Their existence as wild, foraging animals on the moor had truly come to an end and they were back where they belonged, the respected leaders of an ancient, tight-knit community.

Jamie, whose wild dancing and heavy drinking had finally caused him to collapse in the centre of the room, his huge body knocking over the other dancers like a falling tree crushing the small flowers that live in its shade, was being tended on the wooden steps of the house. He came to with a start as the crisp night air pierced his lungs. He was staring into the face of a girl so beautiful he felt sure that he was dreaming.

She was a tiny, delicate creature. Her large, brown eyes sloped upwards at the side, like those of a Highland deer, and her mouth formed a pert bow. Ringlets of warm, auburn hair fell over her forehead and partly covered her high, slanting cheekbones.

Jamie was stunned.

'Why, you're beautiful. Are you real?'

His hand reached out slowly and his fingertips brushed the smooth velvet of her cheeks with a wondering gentleness. She gave a slight start and her movement brought Jamie to his senses.

'Oh, my dear woman, I am so sorry.' He lumbered to his feet, leaning his hand against the front door for support. 'I am sorry if I have offended you. It is the effect of too much good drink. You must forgive me.' His cheeks flushed as red as his beard and his eyes cast desperately about as he attempted to avoid her gaze. Then she laughed. It was a delicious, melodious sound.

Jamie forced himself to meet her eyes. She was smiling up at him, her small lips slightly parted. She shook the hair from her eyes in a motion of the head so wild, free and yet so gentle that Jamie knew that he had at last met a woman to love. He had enjoyed his fair share of infatuations and romantic escapades, but this was so different. This had to be love.

Inside the house, the musicians swept once more into a dancing tune, and the music was strange to Jamie in the cold night air, faint and distant, as adult voices sound to a sleeping child.

The girl spoke. 'Are you better, sir?'

It took a moment for the content of her question to register with Jamie, so intent had he been on the sound of her voice.

'Yes . . . indeed,' he blurted, uncertain of what to say next. 'Then shall we return inside?'

'Yes . . . no! Please don't go yet. Tell me who you are.'

She paused for a moment.

'Yes, that is fair. After all, I know that you are Jamie McIan of Glencoe. I am the sister of the man you have brought back from the dead. My name is Jeannie Gregor.'

'And are you . . . have you a husband?'

'Sir, you are indelicate!' There was gentle mockery in her voice.

Jamie blushed once more. 'I can assure you I meant no

offence. I am as clumsy with words as with my body. I am not, as you must have noticed, a very delicate person. I am built like an ox, and sometimes think I have an ox's brain.' Jamie felt miserable. He would lose this beautiful girl if he was not careful.

Jeannie rose from the step and placed her hand on his arm.

'You are a fine man. Any woman would be proud to have such a great warrior . . . for a husband.'

She stood on tiptoe, pulled his head down with one hand and kissed him lightly on the lips before skipping excitedly back into the house, leaving Jamie alone in the night, his pulse racing, an inexpressible joy welling in his heart.

'For a husband.'

He repeated the words softly, several times, as if to convince himself that he had not misheard.

As the hour of midnight came and went, some of the guests began to leave, for at least ten of them were Gregors from a neighbouring village, situated nearly a mile away across the fields, and soon after they had left, the members of Hugh's own village began to make their unsteady way to their own huts. The old men swayed and staggered and even the women who carried babies showed the effects of drink. It had been a marvellous evening for all of them. When the last of the guests – at least those who had not collapsed – had gone, Hugh Gregor turned from the front door, weary but content, and began to pick his way amongst the sleeping bodies on the floor, making his way towards his own room where he knew his wife was waiting for him.

A hand descended on his shoulder. It was Alasdair, entirely sober. His face was sad.

'Hugh, I realise that this is not the best moment, but we must talk as soon as possible.'

Hugh grinned. 'Better now than that you should burst through my door in the middle of the night. I might be attending to other matters. Oh, don't look so shocked. We Gregors are blunt people at the best of times. And believe me, these are the best of times.'

'Do not fear, Hugh. I am no blushing child. I was just thinking to myself, that but one day past you were near to a wild animal, and look at you now. The change is remarkable and I am deeply happy for you. It is that which makes what I have to say so difficult.'

'Out with it, man.'

'Only when the others are present.'

They found Lindsay Hamish sleeping under the main table and woke him. Jamie, much to their astonishment, was sitting on the steps of the house, staring at the sky with rapt attention. Several of the guests must have tripped over him while taking their departure, but it seemed to have made no difference. Hugh had to resort to a sharp prod in the back to bring him round.

The four men stood, breathing the night air, relishing its cleanness after the oppressive heat of the main room.

Alasdair spoke first.

'Hugh and Lindsay, you have both found happiness here. If you wish to remain while we continue on our way, that is well enough. I shall not bind you to our oath.'

Hugh Gregor stopped him with a sharp gesture.

'Our happiness we owe in full to you. We have sworn an oath and are members of the Devil's Clan. From the moment we met you, we have been whole men once more. Were we to renounce our oath we would once more be incomplete. We joined with you in order to gain revenge on the English. I still intend to exact my revenge. I have told my wife. She is not happy to lose me so soon but acknowledges my obligation.'

Lindsay Hamish followed with some rare words. 'You have made me a man again. For that I would follow you to hell itself.'

Alasdair smiled in the darkness. 'Your guess might be a good one. I believe the Devil to be at Inverness.'

Jamie was puzzled. 'And who can you be thinking of?'

Hugh gave a gasp of surprise as he realised the import of Alasdair's words.

'Yes, Hugh, you have guessed. The man himself.'

Hugh crossed himself.

CHAPTER SIX

THE ATTACK

'Jackson, wake up. Lazy dolt!' Hinchcliffe shook the sleeping man roughly by the shoulder. In the cruelly revealing morning light the Captain no longer cut a dashing figure. He had lost his hat and wig and his uniform was torn and spattered with mud.

'Jackson!' He kicked the redcoat and the body began to stir. Jackson's eyes flickered open. He saw Hinchcliffe and began whimpering. His hands and feet began scrabbling at the ground as he attempted to get away. Hinchcliffe caught him by the collar and restrained his efforts.

'Jackson, you fool. It is me, Hinchcliffe.' A glint of recognition appeared in the man's frightened eyes and his breathing became normal again.

Suddenly Hinchcliffe noticed the mark on his forehead and leaned forward to brush away the dirt that partly obscured it.

'Good God, what's this?'

Jackson tried to speak but could only croak weakly. His lips and throat were parched. The Captain fetched a canteen of water from his saddle, and when he had returned, wet his fingers and passed them over Jackson's dried lips pouring some of the water into the soldier's mouth. At length he was able to speak.

'They did it to me, Captain. They are madmen. They told me no soldier would sleep easy while they were here. I believe them.' His face screwed up, tears came to his eyes and he began to sob uncontrollably.

Hinchcliffe lashed at him with the back of his hand, grasped his collar again and twisted his neck. 'You might be frightened of them, you damned coward, but just remember what I'm capable of. Pull yourself together and let's have some straight answers, or else that mark on your face will spread over your whole body.'

The harsh words had their desired effect. Jackson stiffened and gave his Captain full attention.

'Good. Now tell me, how many of them were there?'

'Four, Captain.'

'Four?' Hinchcliffe roared in disbelief. 'You expect me to believe that four barbarians could reduce a company of twelve English soldiers to this pitiful state. They've turned your damned head, man.'

'There's nothing wrong with my sanity, Captain. I can still see them standing there in the light of the fire. Muttering oaths they were, as if to the Devil. They were like demons.'

'I didn't ask for conjecture, Jackson. Just facts.'

'They pledged themselves to take revenge on the English. One of them nearly killed me, he did. Raised one of them big swords above my head and was ready to use it on my skull only that MacDonald, he stopped him. Honest as I'm sitting here. Then this MacDonald he tried to explain as how they weren't as bad as we'd been led to believe, and how they just wanted to live in peace.'

'Enough of their conversation. If they'd wanted to live in peace they should have stayed at home. How did you get that mark on your head?'

'MacDonald got out a metal crucifix and heated it in the fire. He put it on my head. They had to hold me down. The pain was very bad, Captain, very bad. He said I was to act as a warning to all that came after him.'

Hinchcliffe remained silent, crouched on his haunches for a few moments after the soldier had finished his story. 'I am sure he means every word, but it'll do him little good,' he mused half to himself as his hand toyed with the frayed golden epaulet on his shoulder.

'Who were their new companions?'

'Wild animals, Captain. A fearsome sight with their hair all long down their back. Not human, that's for sure. Gregor, one of them was called. Hugh Gregor. I don't remember any more. I was mighty confused.'

Hinchcliffe snorted his derision. 'Confused, indeed. I intend to get those savages, Jackson, and I intend to do it with your help. Behave well and we'll forget your cowardice. Behave badly, and you'll wish you were back with the Highlanders. Understood?'

Jackson nodded hurriedly, a fresh pang of fear gripping his stomach.

The two men clambered on to Hinchcliffe's horse and galloped off towards Fort William. Within half an hour Fate had smiled on them in the form of a cavalry detachment travelling in the opposite direction, from Fort William to Fort Augustus. The astonished commander was glad to lend six of his riders to Hinchcliffe, and wished his colleague luck before continuing on his way. Within an hour the riders had reached a mean, dirty Highland village on the outskirts of Rannoch Moor. They assembled the townsfolk in the centre of the village. Hinchcliffe chose a dignified elder of the village and a pretty child of about nine years. Soldiers held the old man back while Hinchcliffe worked on the young girl with his knife. He questioned the old man repeatedly, prodding the knife further and further into the girl's flesh. Just when he was sure it would burst the skin and pierce her heart, the man gave in and pointed with a resigned expression, slowly raising a quivering, gnarled hand in a westward direction. Hinchcliffe grinned and stabbed the girl through the heart and gave the order for a general massacre to commence. Some of the old men managed to stagger to the edge of the village before being cut down with swords, and one young boy disappeared into the heather on the north side of the houses, but was soon flushed out. A zealous redcoat beheaded him and carried his trophy back towards the town.

Within minutes the town lay still and dead. The departure of the laughing, exhilarated soldiers was followed by ghastly, lifeless eyes. From one of the huts came the familiar wail of a babe denied its mother's breast to suck.

Jamie was the first to awaken on the morning after the party. His head throbbed and his throat felt as if it had been filled with gravel while he slept, but despite his physical predicament, he felt a deep joy which he could not at first explain. Then it came to him. Jeannie! He smiled and tried to get up, but quickly subsided back on to the table on which he lay. Would he never learn? Brandy and whisky were no good for a man's head when taken together. Like a Campbell and a MacDonald in the same room. Still, it had been a grand night, one of the grandest he had known.

Steeling himself, he whisked his legs off the table and stood up, his muscles tensed and his head buried deep between his shoulder blades. His hands shook and his legs were rubbery as he picked his way through the sleeping figures that still littered the floor. He had noticed a barrel of water outside on the previous day. He opened the main door and shut his eyes tight against the glare of the early morning sun. Creeping out, he shielded his face with his hands and shut the door quietly behind him. He walked to the barrel, full to the brim with rainwater, and after tentatively trickling water over his face with his fingers, plunged his whole head into the barrel and shot it out again with great speed. He suppressed a cry of shock. Good and cold, as God had intended it to be, the freezing water numbed the pain in his head, and he felt much better as he turned to face the sun.

He cast his eyes over the surrounding land. It rolled gently away on all sides. Good farming land, and the fields were well-tended, he noticed with satisfaction. About a hundred yards away, on the eastern side of the village, stood a roebuck, nuzzling at something on the ground. Steam rose from the animal's nostrils. The object of its attention was a vague huddled shape which Jamie could not identify. He decided to investigate. Some brusque walking might steady his legs and create a hearty appetite for breakfast. He thought of slaughtering the deer, but decided to let it live. There had been too much death in these lands already. As he walked towards the animal, he noticed with a strange presentiment of doom that the ground was littered with other objects similar to the one which had engaged the deer's attention. Jamie's heart started beating faster and he broke into a trot. The deer looked up with startled liquid eyes and fled, its long legs a blur in the early-morning sun.

When he was about thirty yards from the object Jamie checked his running. He could now make out what it was. A human body. He began to walk towards it with cautious slowness. It was an old man and one of the guests at the party. The man's eyes stared beseechingly upwards, but he was quite obviously dead. A sliver of dry blood ran from one of the corners of his mouth. His limbs were strangely twisted, jutting out at odd angles from the plaid which covered him. Jamie wondered vaguely whether someone had placed it on his body or whether it had fallen there naturally. Perhaps the old man had pulled the plaid around himself in his death agonies. Jamie lifted a corner of the garment. It revealed an ugly red gash on the dead man's stomach. He let the cloth fall back in place.

As he gazed over the surrounding field, he estimated that there were some fifteen or sixteen other bodies. They were the villagers who had left the celebrations early to walk back across the field to their own homes. Someone had been waiting for them, but who and why? Jamie saw something move from the corner of his eye. The almost imperceptible movement had come from a clump of several bodies some fifty yards beyond where Jamie stood. He stared intently. Perhaps it had been the wind plucking at some clothing, but no, there was another distinct movement.

'Thank God,' he cried and began running towards the bodies. He had hardly begun to move when the shape reared into the air. The redcoat's rifle glinted in the morning sun. Jamie was halfway to the ground when the first shot rang out and dirt spat a mere foot from his arm. He scrambled to his feet and took off in what he hoped was the direction of the house. His long legs took vast strides and the earth seemed to shake beneath him. His heart pumped furiously as shots ricocheted just in front and alongside his lurching frame. Something bit into his leg and he stumbled slightly, but his momentum kept him moving forward. He tripped but bounced up again in a frenzy of fear and determination. As the house loomed in front of him he looked up to see eager, worried faces and bursts of flame from firing pistols.

He launched himself at the door. It opened just as his body was about to hit it and he tumbled into the room, his mad flight halted only by the opposite wall. In a moment Jeannie was leaning over him, cleaning the wound in his leg. The bullet had left a long, half-inch deep furrow and he could see the white glint of bone as he watched Jeannie's handiwork. She ripped a strip off her linen dress and tied it hurriedly around the injured limb, helped him to his feet, shoved a pistol in his hand and propelled him through the women and children who cowered on the floor to the window.

Outside, the King's soldiers had already begun their retreat. Their plan had been either to make a surprise attack on the house, or more likely, as they had allowed nightfall to pass without incident, to attack the Highlanders as they took off on the next stage of their journey. Jamie took deliberate aim and fired. One of the redcoats jackknifed to attention and slumped to the ground close to another of his dead companions. Half a dozen others were running quickly away, turning to fire the odd defensive shot. Alasdair dived for his claymore and with a whooping scream, plunged through the door of the house closely followed by the other members of the Devil's Clan. The three Highlanders raced across the fields, with Jamie hobbling gamely some way behind. They caught up with two of the soldiers almost immediately. As Alasdair whirled one of them round to face him, he recognised him immediately. The ugly wound on the man's forehead caused him to stop for a moment. It was in the shape of a cross. Alasdair grinned maliciously.

'So, my friend, it looks as if you were fated to die after all. You should have heeded my advice.' With terrifying swiftness, he forced the point of his sword into the soldier's gaping mouth. Hugh dispatched his adversary with a nonchalant thrust of his weapon.

In the distance the remaining soldiers had almost reached a clump of horses standing in a neighbouring field. They were obviously beyond capture, and the three Highlanders halted, staring after them, their hands on their knees, wheezing and panting from their exertions. Jamie arrived at the scene, hobbling painfully, blood dribbling from the crude dressing over his wound. When the soldiers had disappeared from view, the four men turned and walked slowly back to the house.

At 6.30 on the morning after the battle at Culloden, the Duke of Cumberland rose from his bed. His head was somewhat painful, but otherwise a sense of immense well-being suffused his spirit.

After the battle he had ridden straight for Inverness. He had occupied the house of Lady Mackintosh, members of whose family were, ironically, serving on both sides of the contest. The mean, dirty capital of the Highlands boasted no finer house, and it appealed to the humorous streak in Cumberland's character, as well as to his overwhelming ego, to inhabit the house his cousin Prince Charles had occupied a few weeks previously. For her former hospitality, the Dowager Lady Mackintosh was immediately incarcerated.

On the previous evening, a grand dinner had taken place. Cumberland had sat at the head of the table, his fat face bathed in sweat and his mouth creased in a near-permanent smile of deep satisfaction. There could no longer be any possible doubt that he, who who had so often been unfavourably compared with his infinitely more dashing cousin, the Bonnie Prince, now had the upper hand . . . and all the glory he could have wished for. As he sat listening to the obsequious and far-fetched praise that poured from his senior officers, hearing himself compared with the greatest military geniuses of history, and not finding himself bested in the comparison, he reflected on the probable reaction of London to the great news of his success. The capital would be turned upside down in celebration of his deeds, and his name would be on everyone's lips. He, William, the child-general, the boy-hero who had saved his country, for had the Highland savages not marched almost to the gates of London? As the brandy fumes began to fog his mind he wondered idly why they had turned back from the brink of certain victory.

'And, sir, what shall happen to the rebels now?' Cumberland thought for a moment.

'What would you recommend we do with the traitors, Colonel?'

The Colonel sat forward in his seat, his face eager. 'Kill them, sir, every one. Wipe them from the land, women and children included. Highlanders are an unruly mob of savages always open to the temptation of traitorous acts against the Crown. Each Highlander killed will represent one less traitor. That, sir, is logic.'

The table was hushed as Cumberland stared for a moment at the officer.

'Sir. That is my kind of logic.'

A roar of laughter welled up from the soldiers, and Cumberland beamed at them, prouder of them at that moment than he had ever been. True, the campaign had not been much to his taste. It contained none of the spirit of proper soldiering which he had enjoyed so much in Flanders, but there was little doubt that it had its compensations. And very handsome ones they were.

The colonel had been right. When he thought of the endless nights without sleep, questioning to himself again and again the ability of his troops to stand up to the kilted beasts who aroused such fear in them, not to mention his own ability as a commander, it made him angry despite his success. That any group of men, let alone these animals, should question his father's right to rule, and that they should go so far as to raise arms against him, why, it was almost unthinkable.

They would pay dearly for their impudence. A hunger for revenge rose in his breast. He knew what his men would be doing to the survivors of the battle at that very moment. In any other circumstances he would have dismissed the wholesale slaughter of defenceless soldiers as inexcusable butchery. But this was different. They had pushed him too far. He reached for the brandy bottle and poured himself a generous measure, eyes bulging with the effort of leaning forward as the table cut into his distended stomach.

'Gentlemen!' He rose unsteadily to his feet. All turned in reverent silence to watch him.

'Let us drink a toast.' His beady eyes searched the faces of his officers. He noted the fear in their eyes and the absence of love. Well, it was not part of a commander's duty to be loved. Fear would do as well.

'To Prince Charles, though he be no prince, and to his brave soldiers, though they be not soldiers. May we send them all to hell, and they rot there in eternity.'

A cheer went up from the crowded room that echoed through the town, reaching into the damp cellars that were soon to hold the broken remnants of the Highland clans.

CHAPTER SEVEN

THE MEETING

'Damn the funeral.'

'Hugh!' Jeannie's face flushed with anger. 'How can you talk in such a way. Have you forgotten your religion?'

'No, my dear, I have not forgotten it, but neither have I forgotten my people. We must not let these murdering bastards escape. My guess is that they have fled to Fort William. We must catch them before they get there.'

'No, Hugh.' Alasdair, who had been listening to the argument, leant forward across the table around which Hugh's family and the other members of the Devil's Clan were seated. 'We have all the time in the world to catch these people. There will be time to bury your dead. I have as great a desire as you to catch up with those soldiers, and one in particular. I think I recognised Hinchcliffe running away from us.'

Jamie nodded quietly. 'I saw him also.'

'Good. So we know our target. Now we have already agreed on our first aim, and we must not be deflected from our purpose despite last night. We will travel east tomorrow morning. We will bury your dead today.'

Eileen placed her hand on Hugh's arm. 'Husband, why will you not tell me what you intend? If you are not chasing after the soldiers, where are you going?' Hugh frowned. He had hoped to get away before his wife and sister could start asking awkward questions. They would have thought him mad had he told them. A group of four Highlanders planning to kill the head of the King's Army. It still sounded a little mad to him, but Alasdair had already got them to agree to the proposal. The Duke of Cumberland was to be made to pay for the crimes of his soldiers. It was good justice, the kind that Hugh could understand, but he could not bring himself to tell Eileen or Jeannie that he was riding to an almost certain death. He shook his head, his mind decided.

'It is best that you remain ignorant for the moment. There

will be time enough for talk when I return.' He paused and looked around the table. 'When we *all* return.' Eileen sighed and sat back, resigned. She knew her husband too well to press him. He was a passionate man of dark moods, with a sharp tongue and a stubborn nature that had often brought him trouble, but he had been a fair and loving husband to her, and his biting wit, which was famous amongst the members of his clan, had never been turned against her. She had been granted most of her requests in life. This was her chance to repay him.

'Hugh, come with us. There will be time for Hinchcliffe later.' Alasdair's voice was anxious. Hugh stared at the table for a moment, and just when Alasdair was sure that he would refuse, nodded his head, albeit somewhat slowly and with more than a hint of reluctance. Alasdair smiled. He only hoped that Cumberland was still at Inverness. For no apparent reason he thought suddenly of his father. That tough old man would have appreciated such a scheme. He shivered at the thought and he could almost feel his father's presence in the room next to him, but resisted the temptation to turn around.

The three Highlanders sat on their horses, impatient to be on their way. Jamie, meanwhile, sat in the main room of the house hastily scribbling on a piece of paper. His letter started 'My dearest Jeannie,' and contained a protestation of love both clumsy and touching. As he wrote, his tongue protruded nervously from the corner of his mouth and his forehead furrowed in concentration. When he had finished, he sprinkled salt on the paper, folded it neatly several times and twisted it round the golden ring which his father had given him on his sixteenth birthday, just weeks before his death. It was Jamie's most precious possession, and it seemed fitting that Jeannie should have it. Then he got up quickly from the table and moved quickly and quietly through the house. When he came to Jeannie's room, he placed the ring carefully on the latch of the door so that it would fall when she opened it and thereby guarantee her attention. 'I will come back for you,' he whispered softly, so as not to wake her. Outside, the others had dismounted, tired of waiting for him. He apologised profusely, but being unable to think of a suitable excuse, gave no explanation.

Hugh and Lindsay were almost unrecognisable. Both had

shaved and Lindsay's hair had been cropped. Hugh had left his long and it fell in wild curls and tangles down the back of his clean jacket. With his beard shaved, the others noticed that his mouth curled up slightly on one side giving him a permanent expression of mild and disdainful amusement. Both Hugh and Lindsay had thrown away their kilts in favour of tartan trews.

'Well, Jamie,' said Alasdair as they mounted their horses afresh, 'I think it very kind of these fashionable gentlemen to ride with such ragged characters as ourselves.' The Gregors laughed good-naturedly.

'Come,' said Hugh, 'I will lead you in the right direction for Inverness.'

Jamie prayed fervently, as the four horses thundered off towards the east, that Hugh would soon be leading them back. He now had something to live for.

Hinchcliffe sat breathing in the rich fumes of the inn's smoking fire. As he poured himself another glass, his drink-befuddled mind reflected on the plan which it had recently hatched. After the attack on Hugh Gregor's guests, and his timely escape from the clutches of Alasdair MacDonald and his companions, Hinchcliffe had been tempted to return to Fort William with the few soldiers left alive under his command, but had changed his mind at the last moment. He had never paid much attention to his career. It had been necessary to undertake some sort of work to ensure a constant supply of money from his father, and he never thought beyond that point. Now, an opportunity had presented itself which he would be foolish to ignore. If Cumberland could be convinced that this small band of Highland ruffians constituted a serious threat to his authority in Northern Scotland, then Hinchcliffe might be able to secure for himself a decent-sized command to root out the miscreants. Not only would this give him a chance to make money out of pilfering and looting, but the Duke's gratitude might be reflected in financial terms, either in the form of a post carrying more money or a direct gift to a zealous servant. Even if the scheme did not work out in full, at least he would get his revenge on Alasdair. Yes, he would enjoy that. For the first time since he had donned a uniform, he had a positive reason to loathe his enemy and a reason for risking his life.

He called loudly for the innkeeper to bring him another bottle of claret.

Now there was only one problem left. How to convince the noble Duke, or rather, how to keep details of his past career away from him. As he started on the second bottle he began to search in his mind for the key to the fat little German's character. Pride? Greed? Envy? No doubt all were present in him, but there had to be something else. Of course! Hinchcliffe could dimly remember being told that as far as Cumberland was concerned this was a private war between himself and his cousin. He would tell Cumberland that Alasdair's little band had been formed by Prince Charles himself with a view to assassinating him if the Rebellion should fail.

It had taken the Highlanders several hours to cut a path through the harsh, treacherous rock of the mountains, and it was late in the afternoon when they finally reached the end of the trail and found themselves at one end of a diminutive loch standing in a plush green valley. Their hearts were gladdened by the sight of trees and the water with the sun reflected in ever-diminishing arcs on its shimmering surface. In the distance a boat floated motionless on the lake.

My God, thought Alasdair, someone is fishing, but when he thought about it a little more deeply, it did not seem so strange, for there was no reason for all normal life to halt as a result of Culloden. He hoped that the man (or woman, for he could not tell at that distance) was faring well. It was good to be reminded of how life had once been. They trotted down to the water's edge and allowed their tired horses to dip their short necks in the cool water for some minutes before resuming their journey. They had not travelled for more than fifty yards when Jamie leant from his saddle and beckoned for Alasdair some ten yards behind, to join him. As he rode up, Jamie placed his index finger to his lips as a sign for silence. He began to talk hurriedly out of the side of his mouth.

'Look ahead.' Thirty yards in front stood two squat rocks on either side of the road. One rock was rounded, the other concave, as if one large stone had been split apart and each of its parts placed several yards from each other.

'Aye, the Traveller's Stones. I know them well.' According to legend the rocks had been designed by an evil giant whose favourite pastime was to wait for unsuspecting travellers to ride between, whereupon he would roll the rounded stone across to its hollowed partner, thereby catching the unfortunate victim in the middle. No true Highlander could pass between without a shiver of apprehension.

'Unless my eyes are losing their power, someone lies in wait for us,' Jamie hissed.

Alasdair did not question his friend's judgement but beckoned for Hugh and Lindsay to join them. As they trotted up, he slid from his saddle, and crouching low, loped off towards the left-hand stone, to which Jamie had pointed. The three other Highlanders kept riding on, reaching the rock as Alasdair began creeping round behind it, his body flat against the stone, dirk clenched between his teeth. His disappearance was soon followed by a loud whooping noise and two strange figures stumbled from their hiding place and fell in front of the horses' hooves. Jamie's horse reared in fright, and as he calmed it, Alasdair came running from behind the stone, the pistol in his hand pointing at the strangers.

They were women, shawls drawn tightly over their heads by trembling fingers, torn, ragged skirts clinging damply to thin legs. Alasdair dropped his gun in surprise and confusion and gaped in astonishment. The Highlanders began to laugh uproariously at his expression.

'So, you've taken to frightening women, Alasdair. It's no proper work for a man, as you well know.' Hugh Gregor's sarcastic remark was too much for Jamie who already had tears of laughter streaming down his cheeks. With a mighty roar he slid helplessly from his saddle and landed with a thud on the ground, but the fall only redoubled his amusement and his huge red face grew redder and redder as he gasped for breath. Even Alasdair, the butt of all this mirth, could not stop himself from laughing good-naturedly, and as he looked around, he noticed with astonishment that even Lindsay Hamish had been unable to contain himself.

Alasdair took a deep breath and walked over to Jamie and helped the giant to his feet. As Jamie wiped his cheeks and brushed himself off, Alasdair turned his attention to the women, who had also regained their feet. With astonishing speed and without a backward glance the females took to their heels, veering off the road down towards the loch. The Highlanders began laughing once more.

'Come back, you fools. We will not harm you,' Alasdair cried after them. 'Poor lassies. They must be very frightened.

Come, forget about them. Let's get on our way.' He turned to his horse, but Hugh Gregor was staring intently at the disappearing figures.

'What is wrong, Hugh?' asked Alasdair.

'I was just thinking that they run well for women,' he mused, apparently to himself. 'Perhaps it is the soldier's boots they seem to be wearing.' Alasdair and Jamie scrambled on to their horses.

'Are you sure, man?' Jamie anxiously inquired as soon as he was seated.

'Yes, just as sure as I have never seen hairier legs on young ladies before.'

In a moment the four horses were thundering down to the water's edge in hot pursuit of the fleeing figures, who had discarded their skirts and shawls to reveal bare chests and tight white trousers. The horsemen were almost upon them by the time they had reached the water. Both splashed feverishly onwards until the water had reached up to their necks.

The Highlanders dismounted in a leisurely fashion and stood by their mounts.

Hugh Gregor's voice rang out in clear English.

'I hope you realise my little friends that no one knows the depth of this loch. The chances are that you would have to travel to the other side of the world to find out.' The two men looked anxiously at each other, now straining to keep their mouths above the water-line. 'And no one knows what manner of beasties lurk down there.'

They both attempted to peer down, eyes opened wide in fear, obviously expecting to feel the suck of a sea serpent's tentacle on their legs at any moment.

'And you will already have noticed that it is a trifle cold in there. They say men do not last very long in such terrible cold.' Hugh Gregor's voice wafted out to them across the water, jagging at their already raw nerves.

They hastened as quick as they could, arms flailing in a desperate attempt to reach the shore before the serpent reached them. They had heard terrible stories about Loch Ness. They did not need reminding of them now.

Hugh smiled cruelly at them as they emerged from the water.

'And is this the bravery your King expects for his generous shilling?'

The two men stood, miserable and foolish, dripping wet and

shivering with a mixture of cold and fear. They were not really men. They were mere boys, neither being more than seventeen years of age. The taller of the two was a handsome boy, although rather starved and pinched-looking. He had large, frightened eyes that threatened to spill with tears. His companion was somewhat squat and big-muscled for his age, with eyes that were no more than slits in his puffy face, and a slack lower lip which gave him a surly demeanour.

Alasdair, who had been scooping the crystal water into his mouth and over his dusty hair, got up slowly from the lake's edge, and, after replacing his bonnet, turned to the boys.

'Last night, my brave soldiers, for I take it that that is what you are, your companions killed ten Highlanders who were friends and relatives of these good gentlemen.' He indicated Hugh and Lindsay, whose backs were turned upon the scene. 'They murdered them in cold blood. I intend to do the same to you, despite your age.'

The taller of the two boys, whose chin had been on his chest throughout the address, fell to his knees, put his head in his hands and began sobbing rhythmically, his body swaying softly back and forth.

The squat boy squinted sideways at him, a sneer of contempt on his lips.

Alasdair remained unimpressed by the performance, sure that it was a trick. 'Jamie, start a fire. We'll brand them after we kill them to let people know that it was we who did it.'

Jamie turned quickly and walked towards some trees further along by the water's edge. Alasdair removed his sword from his belt, and almost nonchalantly testing its sharpness on his fingers, moved slowly towards the youth who knelt on the ground.

'As you are so obliging, youngster, you shall be first.'

As Alasdair raised the sword above his head a faint wind ruffled the locks of hair peeking out from under his bonnet and shivered across the eerily silent lake. He lowered the sword as if in a dream and the breeze died away. The boy at his feet stopped sobbing and looked timorously upwards to discover the cause of the delay in his execution. A look of wonder stole into his eyes as he stared up at Alasdair.

Alasdair was miles away, with Kathy in Glencoe. He remembered the feeling of peace that had engulfed him only a few days previously on the morning before he had set out

67

with Jamie on his quest. It seemed such a long time ago. Perhaps he had dreamed the scene or had read it in a book or heard it from a poet. The water of the lake rippled again and it reminded him of the grass in Glencoe and how it waved gently when the wind blew softly across it.

A twig snapped nearby as Jamie searched for wood for the fire and Alasdair was awakened from his reverie. He lifted the claymore once more.

'NO!' The cry tore into the silence. Alasdair glared down at the boy. He gasped and the sword slipped from his hands and clattered noisily on the stones that ringed the lake-shore. He was staring into the eyes of the boy who had begged for his life to be spared that night by the campfire. The very boy who had refused to slice off the old lady's finger in Alasdair's village.

The boy's squat companion stared at the scene in amazement, and Hugh and Lindsay turned round to find out what was happening. Soon the ground shook at the approach of Jamie, no less surprised to see Alasdair's reticence.

Hugh Gregor strode up to Alasdair and spun him round.

'And what is wrong now? Have you lost your resolve after all that you have told us? Does the sight of an innocent face blind you to the crimes its owner has most likely been responsible for? If you've changed your mind then leave the work to me.' Hugh bent quickly to reclaim the sword.

Alasdair spoke softly, his eyes still fixed on the boy. 'That will not be necessary, Hugh. I would rather you killed me than take this boy's life.'

The Highlanders crouched around the fire watching the boys eat.

'What is your name?' asked Hugh, staring at the taller of the youths. He looked up, somewhat apprehensively.

'Tom, sir, and this here's Billy,' he said, indicating his squat companion. Billy grunted non-committally and continued eating voraciously.

Hugh pondered for a moment. 'And what are those dreadful scars on your back?' The plaid which Jamie had kindly placed across the boy's shoulders had slipped as he shovelled food into his mouth. His back bore the marks of countless striped lacerations, some nearly healed, others quite fresh.

'From flogging, sir.'

'What did you do to deserve that? It must have been something wicked,' suggested Alasdair.

'No, sir, at least I did not think it so. I had become very fond of one of the girls who followed the camp. Only young she was, but pretty, and not like the others.' Billy grunted disbelievingly. Tom flushed and continued. 'Well, sir, we had decided to become wed and I went to ask permission of my colonel, and that was that.'

'What do you mean?' prompted Hugh.

'Well, sir, he ordered me 100 lashes.'

'What for?'

'Impertinence, sir.'

The Highlanders looked at each other incredulously.

'But surely a man may marry whom he chooses.'

The muscular boy spoke, morsels of meat spitting from his mouth.

'The girls that follow the camp are whores. The officers don't like their men marrying whores . . . though half the men are riddled with the pox.'

'Good God, boy, why did you join in the first place?'

Tom thought for a while before replying. 'I was born near Lincoln and had lived my whole life on my father's farm. Life was hard and there seemed no escape. Then one day the soldiers were billeted in a nearby village, and I saw them marching past the farm. Those "lobsters" looked so fine and manly in their red uniforms, and I got to thinking about the countries they would probably visit and the romantic lives they would lead, and so I got up early one morning, spoke not a word to my family, walked to the village and joined. I was but fifteen then. That was two years ago. I would give anything to be back on my farm now.' An earnest expression came into the boy's eyes.

Alasdair turned to Billy. 'And how did you come to join, my young friend?'

'Pressed into the service, sir. Standing late one night outside an inn in Holborn, waiting for my father. A gang of redcoats came round the corner, and began to converse with me. Before I knew what was happening, they had me unconscious and trussed up neat and tidy. I was fourteen, but looked older.'

'And have you too suffered the lash?'

'Only once, sir.' The boy was silent, obviously unwilling to expand on the statement.

Alasdair continued his questioning. 'And was it so terrible you cannot speak about it?'

'I do not like to think about it, but I will tell you.' A harsh look crept into his eyes. 'I had lost some money gambling with friends and needed some pennies urgently. They had threatened to beat me unless I paid them back. I sold my bread ration to a friend. An officer found out and they were going to execute me for it, but luckily our commander is a kindly man. I took the alternative punishment.'

'And what was that?'

'Five hundred lashes.'

Alasdair whistled softly between his teeth. No wonder the British soldiers were so brutal. They learnt the art of inhumanity from masters.

'And do you wish to go back, Billy?'

'Is there any other course open to me?'

'Yes!' Alasdair paused for a moment. 'Join us.'

The two boys gawped in astonishment, and Billy began to laugh.

Hugh had jumped angrily to his feet. 'Man, you are crazy! English in the Devil's Clan? You may as well send a letter to Cumberland asking him to join.'

Alasdair continued to stare at the boys. Tom was the first to speak. 'Yes, sir, I will join gladly.' Hugh, beside himself with rage, stormed off towards the lake shore.

'And you, Billy?'

The boy nibbled reflectively at a bone. 'If Tom is willing to join you, then so am I.'

'Good,' cried Alasdair and got to his feet and went off in pursuit of Hugh.

Hugh turned with obvious anger on Alasdair when he had caught up with him. 'This is very fine, I must say. Englishmen in the Clan. Recent events have obviously affected your reason.'

Alasdair put his arm around Hugh's shoulder. 'Now, listen to me for one minute. What else could we do? We cannot send them back to their regiment and that sort of cruelty. Neither of them wishes to go in any case. There is no chance of them reaching their homes without meeting the army, and anyway, they are both deserters. They will be executed if caught. That young boy saved my life back there on Rannoch. Had he not delayed Hinchcliffe for those precious minutes your intervention would have come too late. I have to repay him. You must see that.'

Hugh remained sullen and unconvinced. 'For your sake, Alasdair, I will agree, but not until I have seen them prove their willingness to fight in our cause.'

'Very well, friend, what would you have them do?' Hugh thought for a moment, and then he smiled a wicked smile.

'We will ask them to kill a redcoat each. If they hate their own army so much there should be little problem. If they refuse, then we can set them loose. They will be in no worse a position than when we found them.'

CHAPTER EIGHT

THE REVENGE

The two soldiers stood for a moment outside the door of the inn, stunned by the cold of the night. Their minds were reeling and their bowels were in violent upheaval. They stumbled to the back of the building and relieved themselves hurriedly, then buttoned their uniforms and stood leaning against the building, exhausted. The strong Highland ale had done its work and both were paying the penalty for their greed.

As they pushed themselves away from the wall, two shadows flitted momentarily through the dim light coming from the window at the back of the inn. The first soldier moaned as the knife entered his back. He fell forward to his knees and gurgled as he subsided on to the ground.

'Harry? You not finished yet?' The older soldier walking some paces in front of his companion, giggled, but the sound stopped short as a knife cut a red gash through his windpipe. His fingers scrabbled at his throat as his lungs caved in, airless.

Billy wiped his knife on his plaid as Tom turned over the body of the first soldier. The man's grimacing face was just visible in the light from the window.

'God, Billy. I know this man. He's a dragoon I shared a brandy with before Culloden. He was a kindly soul.' The boy's delicate face filled with anguish and tears sprang to his eyes.

'Come, Tom. We've seen enough dead men in our time. This is not the place to start acting like a woman.' Tom jumped to his feet and lashed out at his companion, knocking him to the ground.

'Don't call me that, or so help me, you will soon end up like them.' Tom pointed a quivering finger at the dead soldiers, while Billy lay on the ground, rubbing his jaw where Tom's fist had made contact. They stared threateningly at each other.

Suddenly the tension was broken by a familiar voice.

'Shut up, damn you. I am attempting to sleep in here.'

A figure had appeared at the low window. The two boys froze where they were.

'Get back in here at once, or I'll have you flogged when we reach Fort Augustus. And don't believe I can't do it.'

The figure moved away from the window and the boys breathed deep sighs of relief.

'Did you recognise the voice?' Billy whispered urgently.

'How could I forget it. I feel as if a beetle had just crawled up my spine.'

The two boys bolted into the night.

Inside the inn, Hinchcliffe returned to his chair which was placed in front of the heavily-smoking fire.

'Innkeeper,' he roared. There was no reply.

He got out of the chair and staggered towards the flimsy partition which separated the main part of the inn from the owner's quarters. As he made his way across the room his head smashed into the low roofbeam that supported the small house. He thumped it with his hand in anger and the building shook dangerously.

The innkeeper, terrified for his property, scurried from behind the partition.

'Yes, sir. Can I help you?'

'Where have you been, you lazy dog? My throat is raw. I want some more of that fine French claret. At least there is something to recommend in this damnable country.' Hinchcliffe suddenly grew suspicious. His eyes focused on a spot beyond the innkeeper's shoulder. 'What have you got back there, I wonder, that demands so much of your attention?' he said, pointing at the partition. 'What are you hiding back there, you little turd of a man?'

He lurched towards the partition, knocking aside the weakly protesting innkeeper. The living quarters consisted of two crude box-like beds at floor-level and little else. Huddled in the corner were three children, half-naked, barefoot and covered in grime. Their eyes were red-rimmed from the smoke that filled the whole room and mucus ran freely from their nostrils. They clung fearfully to their mother, a striking, red-haired woman of not more than twenty-five years of age. Her eyes held the sad patience born of great suffering.

Hinchcliffe's eyes bored into her, but she stared at the floor, not daring to meet the Englishman's gaze. He laughed unpleasantly. 'Well, so it is you he has been hiding from me all evening.' He walked over to the corner in which the family

73

huddled, and bending down, reached out his hand to stroke her cheek. 'What fair skin. You red-headed whores are usually made of old leather. No, my dear, you have certainly been wasted here . . . until now.' He grabbed her hair and yanked her to her feet. The woman's sad eyes flashed in hatred and her nails slashed down the side of the Captain's face, drawing blood. He laughed excitedly, and turning her away from him, clasped her around the waist, lifting her small body off the ground, so that the flailing arms and legs had no effect. The children, thrown back by the violence of Hinchcliffe's attack, now returned to harry his legs. The eldest, a boy of about seven years, raced to the other side of the room and rushed towards Hinchcliffe with a meat cleaver clasped in his tiny hands, hardly able to lift the murderous instrument from the ground. As he struggled to raise it above his head, Hinchcliffe turned quickly round and watched as the instrument swung towards the boy's mother. The horrified child, unable to curtail the momentum of his swing, wailed in anguish as the cleaver cut into her leg.

The woman screamed as blood spurted from the wound. The Captain aimed a mighty kick at the boy's head, endangering his own balance, and caught the child square in the temple, killing him instantly. The other two children crawled to their dead brother, and after staring at him for some seconds in shock, reached out tentatively to touch his dead body.

Hinchcliffe's eyes blazed with excitement as he dragged the feebly-struggling woman towards the partition.

'We'll have to get you outside to cool your temper, whore,' he grunted as he dragged her around the partition into the main part of the inn. 'There is still time for some amusement.'

A voice stopped him. 'I fear that time has run out for you, my friend.'

Hinchcliffe gasped and let go of the woman, wheeling to face the intruder. Her body slumped noisily to the floor.

Alasdair MacDonald stood just inside the open door of the inn, a pistol in his hand trained on Hinchcliffe's head. The astonished Englishman gaped stupidly. His hand dropped to his own pistol as Alasdair fired. The ball hit Hinchcliffe's arm, cutting a furrow in the skin above the bicep muscle of his left arm. He clutched at the wound and dropped to his knees.

Alasdair pointed to the bleeding woman.

'Take her and tend to her wounds, Innkeeper. She is losing much blood.' The man stumbled to his wife, and with a struggle, managed to pick her up and carry her behind the partition. They heard him muttering a prayer.

There was a click behind Alasdair, followed by a pistol crack. One of the soldiers at the table had awakened and fired at the Highlander. The ball thudded into the turf wall, inches from Alasdair's head, and as he turned, he launched himself at the soldier. As they grappled on the floor, Hinchcliffe drew his dagger from his belt, and still clutching his arm as best he could, crawled on his knees towards the struggling pair. As he passed the open door of the inn a foot protruded from the darkness and thudded into his ribs, sending him sprawling, face-downwards. He tried to look up, but a huge brogue shoe pressed savagely into the back of his neck. Alasdair rolled away from the soldier he had been fighting. The redcoat lay with a dirk sticking into his heart. As Alasdair sat gasping on the floor, the last redcoat leapt from his seat and plunged towards the door. He had been crouched below the line of the round table to escape detection. Jamie, whose heavy foot was holding Hinchcliffe firmly in place, watched the fleeing figure quizzically. No sooner had the soldier disappeared through the door than a high-pitched scream was heard. Hugh Gregor and Lindsay Hamish entered the inn, sheathing their swords.

They stood for a moment to survey the scene. All was silent apart from the soft moaning of the innkeeper's wife from behind the partition and Alasdair's heavy breathing. The Highlander shook his head and drew trembling fingers through his hair before reaching out a hand to retrieve the bonnet which had been knocked off during the struggle.

He glanced up at Hinchcliffe, and getting to his feet, spoke softly. 'Tie him to a chair.' His voice was menacing.

Jamie clasped the Captain under his armpits from behind and dragged him to his original seat in front of the fire.

Hugh looked around for some rope, but unable to find any, disappeared into the innkeeper's quarters. He returned in a moment with some cord.

'I don't suppose I need ask which person was responsible for that, do I?' he said quietly gesturing behind him. Hinchcliffe chortled. 'I did not have any such problems with Mrs Mac-Donald, I can assure you.' Alasdair, unable to contain himself, leapt at the Captain with a snarl of rage, locking his hands around his throat. Hinchcliffe's hands clawed feebly at Alasdair's arms, but it was no use. The Highlander was possessed with the strength of a madman. The Englishman's cheeks began to turn blue and his tongue started to protrude from his mouth as he fought desperately for breath. Just when his head had started threshing frenziedly first to one side and then the other, and his eyes seemed ready to burst from their sockets, Alasdair loosened his grip and took several paces backwards, leaving the Englishman to fall forwards in his seat, sobbing and choking, his hands around his neck as he tried to restore the circulation of blood.

Alasdair, once more composed, stared at him with seemingly passionless detachment as Jamie began to tie up the Captain.

At length Alasdair spoke, his voice calm. 'You can imagine, Captain Hinchcliffe, that I have lain awake the last few nights imagining what I should do to you when we met. Some of my thoughts, I will admit, now seem shameful to me when I reflect on them. But they say it takes a disciple of the Devil to bring forth devilish thoughts, and that you have certainly done.'

Hinchcliffe raised his eyes to look at Alasdair and then he grinned horribly. 'Go on, damn you, kill me. At this very moment I seem to have no fear of death, you will be disappointed to hear.'

'As you know for which region you are bound,' interrupted Hugh, 'it must take away some of the worry.'

'And who in God's name are you, sir?' asked Hinchcliffe.

'Surely you remember me from Rannoch Moor. You were not so eager to die then, as I recall. Ten of my clan lie dead on your account. My name is Gregor. I should like you to know that before you die.'

Hinchcliffe laughed. 'My humblest apologies. I did not recognise you looking so much like a . . . gentleman, if that word could be applied to one of your kind. As for your clansmen, I'm surprised it was so few, but perhaps that was just the enjoyment of killing them impairing my logical faculties. As for your name, it is of no consequence. Barbarians have no use for them, and there will soon be no MacDonalds or Gregors in these parts. The Duke will, I assure you, see to that.'

Silence followed his remarks, and all eyes turned to Alasdair.

'We are not going to kill you.' Alasdair's words made his companions gasp, and Hinchcliffe's remarkably calm exterior began to crack.

'What do you mean?' he shouted, struggling for the first

76

time to free himself from his bonds.

Alasdair grimaced, and Jamie recognised the frighteningly cruel look he had seen several times before on his companion's face.

'No, sir,' continued Alasdair, his voice cold and metallic, 'as you seem so willing to meet your death, and as you have been deliberately provoking us in the hope that it might prove a quick and painless one, I shall change my plans.'

Hinchcliffe was now moving violently and was in danger of breaking the rope.

'Restrain him, Jamie.' Alasdair turned to Hugh and Lindsay. 'If any of you object to anything I might do, please leave, for I shall not be stopped.' The two men nodded. Alasdair walked to the smoking fire, drew out his dirk and plunged it into the embers.

'Do you remember what you promised to do to me that night on Rannoch? Indeed, you would have done it had it not been for the timely appearance of my two comrades.'

A terrible look of fear crept into Hinchcliffe's eyes and his chin began to quiver. Alasdair turned swiftly and caught the panic in the man's expression.

'Oh, do not worry. I have no intention of scalping you. I could not conceive of committing so barbaric an act.' Hinchcliffe looked slightly relieved.

'No,' continued Alasdair. 'As the right of revenge falls on me, I have three wrongs to right. My wife, my father and my son.' Alasdair's voice cracked as he finished talking, and he buried his head in his free hand, momentarily overcome by the memory of his dead family.

Presently he composed himself. 'It is not fitting that one with so scarred a soul should not carry the sign of it on his body. Hell will be waiting for you no matter when you die. I should like you to experience some of it first in this life.'

He paused. The room was quite silent.

'For the three wrongs you have done me, I shall do three wrongs to you, minor in comparison. For your wrong to my wife, I shall brand you with the sign of the cross. You will already have seen the effects on one of your own men.' So saying he withdrew the metal crucifix from his pocket and placed it in the fire next to his dirk. 'For the wrong to my father, you will lose an ear, and for the wrong to my Clan, you will lose an eye.'

A curious choking noise came from Hinchcliffe's throat.

'You will have paid cheaply, but wherever you travel in these Highlands, people will point at you and whisper your shameful story. Your companions in England will shun you for your hideous disfigurements and the young ladies will no longer lie with you, unless it be whores ill with the pox. No, your life will be quite different from now on, and you will often wish that we had killed you.'

Alasdair slowly drew the knife and the crucifix from the fire and moved towards Hinchcliffe who had begun to shriek in horror at his fate. Jamie leant forward to restrain him.

In a minute Alasdair had finished. He had thrown the ear on to the fire and the room was filled with the putrid smell of burning flesh. Hinchcliffe was slumped forward in his chair, an ugly mess where his right ear had been, and a line of blood trickling from his left eye. His tortured whimpers mingled with the moans of the innkeeper's wife.

The four Highlanders stood looking down at their victim, each savouring the knowledge of a wrong righted. Alasdair bent and cut the ropes, and grabbing Hinchcliffe by the collar, propelled him to the door and threw him out into the night. He stood and watched the wrecked man crawl away into the blackness. He felt a strong impulse to run after him and finish him off, but decided to let him live on in his misery.

'And tell that butcher Cumberland that we come for him. The Devil's Clan has not even begun its work.'

He turned and walked back into the inn.

The Highlanders sat by the table while the innkeeper served them food and claret. 'Some nice partridge for you. I was saving it, but as you have undoubtedly saved us, you may have it.'

Billy and Tom silently entered the room and took their places at the table.

'And how is your wife?' asked Hugh.

'Oh, she will limp a little, but she will live and that is the most important thing.'

Alasdair wondered if he was correct in that assumption. Perhaps the Highlands could live on, crippled and humble, but was there any point in such an existence? He pulled some meat from the game bird and drank some wine to wash away the taste of revenge which for some reason had gone sour in his mouth.

They heard hoofbeats approach the inn, and began instinctively to rise from the table.

A crazed, maniacal voice called out to them through the night.

'Damn you. You let me live, damn you, and that was a mistake. You will all rot in hell, but first you'll rot here. Nothing will stop me. Prepare to die, you Highland scum.'

The hoofbeats clattered away, accompanied by the word 'die' echoing eerily on the wind.

Jeannie turned from her knitting and picked up the ring which Jamie had left for her. She fondled it gently, staring at the bright gold and smiled to herself. In the dark, bad days following the death of her clansmen and the loss of her brother so soon after the ecstatic joy occasioned by his unexpected return from Rannoch, she had thought often of Jamie; of his good, broad shoulders, his merry laugh, his huge bushy beard and cheerful eyes and the way he had looked at her on the fateful night of her brother's welcome party. She remembered his wild, passionate dancing, and his drinking! Well, there was no man worth anything that did not like to drink.

She returned to her knitting but threw it down within seconds and drew from a pocket in her dress a crumpled, dirty piece of paper which she unfolded and smoothed lovingly against her thigh.

She read it for the hundredth time.

'My dearest Jeannie,

I am not much of a one for words as you may have guessed, so you must make allowances for any clumsiness of expression on my part. My message is simple in any case. I love you dearly and will take you for my wife, if you should consent to accept me. I knew last night when you came to see me on the steps of this very house that I loved you and thought – I may have imagined it – that my passion found companionship in your own sweet eyes. I shall be back soon, when certain matters are dealt with, and shall expect your answer then. Please, I beg you, let it be yes. For now, please accept this ring and remember me by it – if, indeed, you wish to do so.

Your adoring Jamie.'

She stared at it for some minutes, then folded and replaced

it in her pocket before returning with a sigh and a slight shake
of her head once more to her knitting.

As the first light of dawn crept through the murky windows of
the small inn, the lady of the house rose painfully from her
bed and hobbled to the door.

The morning was beautiful, cold, crisp and clear. It smelt
clean after the clogged, stifling atmosphere of her sleeping
quarters, and as she stood savouring the sweetness of the air,
she momentarily forgot the dull throbbing pain in her leg.
Presently it impinged on her consciousness, and when she gazed
down, she noted that the bandage was soaked with blood. She
decided to wash it in the burn which ran between her house
and their village, whose huddled dwellings she could just make
out through the birch trees on the other side of the stream.

She was happy, despite her intense discomfort. Her honour,
indeed her life, had been saved by the brave Highlanders, who
she had been sad to find had left her house in the small hours
of the morning. As she thought of them she could not help
remembering Hinchcliffe and blinked in an attempt to eradi-
cate his face from her mind, but despite her efforts she could
still see the madness burning in his eyes and could hear the
terrible threats he had screamed at them after his torture.

She shuddered and set off for the stream at a determined
pace. Her poor husband would be in sore need of his breakfast
when he awoke and she had cows and goats to milk before she
could begin cooking it.

As she knelt by the burn, she offered a short prayer to God,
asking that the intruders be banished from her homeland, but
there seemed little use in it. It was obvious that God had finally
decided to punish the Highlanders for their wicked ways. But
why, she wondered, had he chosen the English, of all people,
as the instrument of retribution? She winced as she unwound
the bandage and began cupping handfuls of cleansing water
to the terrible gash in her leg.

There were hoofbeats in the distance. She listened carefully
and counted at least four horses. Perhaps the Highlanders had
returned already. She hoped so, for she had not had a chance
to thank them for their gallantry.

She stood up carefully, keeping the weight from her
wounded leg, and craned her neck to find out who was approaching. Out of the morning mist rode five horses bearing

red-coated soldiers. Dragoons. She inhaled sharply and dropped to the ground, flattening herself against the earth.

The riders slowed to a halt and she could hear the sound of hurried conversation, followed shortly by dismounting noises. She raised her head a few inches and peeped over the bank of the burn. The soldiers were standing still, flaring torches in their hands. She watched, horrified, as they dispersed to various parts of the house. At a signal from their leader, who remained standing some fifteen yards from the front door, the men dragged the flames over the surface of the building, allowing the fire to lick almost lovingly over the turf and wood. Smoke was soon swirling in thick, effulgent layers until the whole house became almost invisible. The woman stifled a cry as her husband, the children clasped desperately to his legs, came tottering from the house, coughing violently, his eyes streaming tears.

The leader of the group stepped forward as his men rejoined him. 'We have instructions to destroy your house and to kill its occupants.' His voice was harsh.

'By whose orders?' shouted the terrified innkeeper.

'By the express order of Captain Hinchcliffe of Kingston's Horse. He asked me to bid you farewell and to tell you that a promise made by him is most certainly a promise kept.'

When the soldier had finished he removed his pistol from his belt and ordered his men to do the same. He raised his left arm in the air and let it drop suddenly. The pistols fired in unison. The innkeeper and the two children lay dead, blood seeping gently from their bullet wounds.

The woman acted before shock could paralyse her. She splashed swiftly over the shallow burn, her wound forgotten, and ran to the nearby village. She re-appeared moments later on a short-limbed Highland horse, which she rode across the stream, up the bank and straight towards the astonished soldiers, who had not even enough presence of mind to fire at her as she galloped past.

Their leader was the first to recover.

'Come, men, after her. It's the woman the Captain told us about. See the wound in her leg.'

They leapt to their horses and were quickly giving chase down the narrow valley that led away from the inn. The woman had set off at a furious pace, crashing her good leg into her animal's side. The horse snorted and slavered, with steam pouring off his back as she spurred him on to greater efforts, but despite his surprising speed, the soldiers were gaining on her with alarming ease. She kept twisting her head round to note their progress.

When she had reached the flattest part of the valley floor and her horse looked to be almost exhausted, as she pulled his head to the right and made him describe a time-wasting arc which brought the soldiers within firing distance.

Then with astonishment, the soldiers saw her bring the animal to a sudden halt. She dismounted swiftly and turned to face the fast-approaching enemy. The riders realised too late why she had taken the detour. Their horses, which had been galloping at breakneck speed, came to a juddering halt, their long legs kicking furiously up and down as they sank into the treacherous bog. The gently undulating surface was soon up to their necks, sucking the hysterical animals inexorably downwards. The riders, their screams of fear mixing with the agonised whinnies of their mounts, scrambled up and placed their boots on the twisting backs of their animals and tried to leap for safety, but all solid ground seemed to have disappeared, and their boots, with sucking and splashing noises, entered the hungry softness of the deceptive ground. Their crazed scramblings only increased the speed of their descent.

Two of the riders managed to grab hold of each other, one hanging grimly to the other's coat-tails while the first got a hand on the solid turf at the edge of the bog. As the dragoon smiled in relief, a bare foot came smashing down on his hand. Just before he slipped away to his death he looked up to see the scowling face of the woman who had but minutes previously been his quarry.

She stood watching, her legs slightly parted, her hands resting on her hips, eyes ablaze with hatred. She continued to stand there until the shouts of the dying men had been silenced, and the ground had stopped bubbling, and all that remained of the murderers were a number of pretty soldiers' bonnets and a limp hand that stuck obscenely out of the placid mud.

As the woman stood, tears came to her eyes, and she turned slowly away and with an air of infinitely sad resignation urged her horse to rise from the ground where he had been recovering from his exertions.

She trotted back up the valley, head bent, her eyes now blind to the beauty of the day.

CHAPTER NINE

THE PLAN

With a howl of mortification Tom ripped the tartan cloth which was wrapped around his limbs from his body, threw it on the ground and stamped on it petulantly.

He stood, half-naked, perplexed and wondering how on earth anyone could have thought of dressing in such a ridiculous fashion. The Highlanders laughed, and Billy joined in gladly having recently been the butt of their mirth.

'I do not know why you are laughing at me,' cried Tom. ' 'Tis we should find you amusing. This costume is fit only for a woman.' He kicked at the cloth

'Come, come, no need for temper, young Tom,' cooed Alasdair, rising from the ground. 'It is not as hard as it seems, and you'll find it mighty comfortable when it is on by your own hand. More comfortable than when someone else fixes it. We have done it for you until now, but we cannot keep doing it. Here, watch me once more.'

Alasdair collected up the cloth, and as if by magic, had fixed it several times around his waist and over and under his shoulder in no time, pinning it by his neck with a flourish when he had finished. The boy meekly accepted the plaid when Alasdair had unravelled it and set about once more to master its entwining mysteries. Thank God, Tom reflected, that he still had his boots and trousers.

Since their meeting by the lake shore a few days previously, Alasdair, with the aid of his colleagues, had attempted to teach the two boys Highland ways, and had achieved some success. They could eat the food without difficulty, and drink the Highland ale without the violent effects suffered by most foreigners. They had even managed to take it from the coif, the flat, two-handled, shallow dish that tended to leave most of its contents in the inbiber's lap. And the boys had listened with wrapt attention to tales of Fingal and the other great heroes of the Highland past, even though Alasdair had found it difficult to communicate the magnificence of the stories in any but the Gaelic tongue. As for Gaelic, Alasdair had decided not to even try teaching it to them. It was a difficult enough language for scholars of foreign tongues, and for two untutored boys it might prove impossible.

At last Tom managed to pin the plaid at his shoulder, but the uneven distribution of the cloth caused the brooch to snap open and the tartan descended to his ankles. This time even he joined in the laughter as Jamie rose to help him once more.

Alasdair, watching the scene, felt a twinge of self-reproach. Was it right to teach these young men a way of life that, as he now fully realised, might not exist within a few years? Was it fair to enlist their aid in a cause that was dying? But what had been the alternative? Alasdair remembered with some guilt that he had been quite ready to lop off their heads. He looked at Tom and shuddered, for there was in the boy a youthful innocence that would have made such an act a crime.

And then Alasdair thought of Angus his own son and realised that the killing, no matter how cruel, would have been justified. Had Tom and Billy, after all, not been present at the event, despite their obvious unwillingness?

He cleared his head of complicated thoughts and concentrated on the job ahead. At first he had desired merely the death of Hinchcliffe and his cronies, but his ambitions had grown to include any English soldier in the Highlands, and then it had become clear to him that all the death and suffering meant little without the death of one particular soldier.

Alasdair moved to the pot of stew that bubbled some yards from him and laconically began to stir it. Cumberland, that monstrous butcher, would have to be assassinated if the word justice was to have any meaning in the future.

'Come on boys,' he called, just as Tom had donned the plaid once more, this time with complete success.

'We must eat and there are still many miles between us and Inverness.'

He watched the two boys as they scooped the rich-smelling food on to wooden plates. They ate greedily. That was good, thought Alasdair. It was the last time they would dare stop to prepare elaborate meals before they had tracked their quarry. He decided then and there, that whatever happened at Inverness, he would give the boys whatever money he had with him and send them south to their own country, where they at least had a chance of a normal life.

In Inverness much comment was aroused by the arrival of a soldier whose face was severly mutilated. It was not his eye or his ear that excited interest, however, for Inverness was, during the period following the massacre at Culloden, a city of missing limbs and hideous deformities, but the sign of the cross which the soldier carried on his forehead looking for all the world as if it had been burned into his skin. Rumours raged concerning the meaning of the sign. Some claimed that it had been placed there by God himself, either as a warning to the English that he was displeased with them or as a sign that he was on their side, depending whether or not the rumour-monger was a Jacobite.

Soon, a new and altogether more likely rumour emerged, one which filled the Jacobites with delight. A small gang of Highlanders, part of the force defeated at Culloden, had decided to exact their revenge on the wicked English, and this was their mark, a warning to all that came after them. Given hope by this admittedly slender proof of a resistance movement, some of the Jacobites went so far as to unlock their special drinking glasses to toast the health of the Young Pretender, wherever he might be.

For the officer. inside the town, however, the stories held no terror, for so convinced were they of their own superiority and of the mendacious character of the Highlander, that they did not for a moment believe in the superstitious tales of avenging warriors. They put the stories down to the effects of whisky drinking.

But one man was beginning to believe the story, and he just happened to be the most important man in Inverness.

The Duke of Cumberland leant back in his chair and pressed his fingers together in what could have been mistaken for an attitude of devotion. His brow furrowed as he listened to the strange report of the deformed man sitting across from him. Hinchcliffe's story was nearly at an end. So far his exaggerated version of recent events had swelled the ranks of the Devil's Clan to twenty and the number of soldiers lying dead on their account to over fifty. He realised the figures would be beyond checking for several weeks at least, and the Duke would have laughed to be informed that his father's Kingdom was threatened by four savage ruffians, whereas the figure twenty had about it an air of respectability.

When Hinchcliffe approached the subject of Alasdair Mac-Donald's threats upon Cumberland's person, the young Duke's eyes opened wide in perceptible disbelief.

'Upon my person!' he spluttered. 'Is he serious? Twenty illiterate cave-dwellers against the might of this army. How preposterous!'

The Duke was beginning to lose interest, and Hinchcliffe saw in his bored expression his chance slipping away. He gambled everything on a huge lie.

'Sir, I realise that it would be difficult to take seriously such a threat from a band of ordinary Highlanders, but Alasdair MacDonald is certainly not that.'

Cumberland's heavy eyelids narrowed and his eyes flickered across Hinchcliffe's face. 'Well, Captain?' Hinchcliffe had managed to reawaken his flagging attention.

'This MacDonald, sir, is a personal friend of King Louis of France, and has been sent by him in secret with the sole aim of killing you. MacDonald has undergone a rigorous course of training organised by the finest officers in Louis' command. I think it would be prudent to accord his plan some respect if only to ensure the capture of this villain in order to humiliate his master.'

Cumberland's eyes had hooded over again during Hinchcliffe's revelation and he sat in silence for fully two minutes, his breath whistling through his nostrils. Hinchcliffe offered up a silent prayer.

'In heaven's name, sir, why should he wish to assassinate me?'

Hinchcliffe was ready for him.

'He did not wish to give military support to the rebel cause when he knew that his troops would be facing men under your own very able command. Now that you have been victorious, he argues, you will have less reason to worry about your personal safety and will therefore present an ideal target. When you are killed the English army will be in disarray and much disheartened by this reversal in their fortunes. It is then that he plans to land his own troops, at the moment of our country's greatest weakness. He does not believe, and I think that most of your loyal officers would agree with him, that our army is capable of victory without your beneficent guidance.'

The young officer rose with much puffing and grunting and

leant across his desk, staring directly into Hinchcliffe's frightened eyes.

'Well, sir, and what do you propose we do about it?'

Hinchcliffe's prayer had been answered, but by whom he could not be sure.

Inverness was the major centre of Highland life. It was the place where clansmen could bring their beef, wool and malt to be exchanged for books, broadswords, pistols and lace. Despite its importance, it was a mean, dirty, small town that rarely boasted more than 3,000 inhabitants. The trading centre consisted of four main roads, three of which met at the Cross, where most of the bartering between Highlander and merchant went on. The houses on the outskirts of the town were the small, huddled turf dwellings to be found throughout the country. The main houses of the town were made of rough stones of various shapes and sizes, covered with a thick layer of mortar. These buildings were no more impressive inside. Separate floor levels were distinguished by one layer of thin planks, as were the partitions between rooms on the same level. Even the major buildings – the Tolbooth, Town Hall and the Coffee House which stood at the Cross – were not particularly remarkable structures and were almost bereft of furniture. To add to the depressing aspect of the town, almost every inch of space, every surface, every corner was filled with dirt. Filth covered every item of furniture, all the food utensils, and was heaped in the corners of the rooms and spread over the narrow, grimy streets.

As a resting place for conquering heroes, it left much to be desired, but as a strategic centre, it was vital. It was the town from which the Highlands could be effectively crippled. It was also of great importance to Alasdair MacDonald, for inside the town, guarded on all sides by his troops and surrounded by his officers, sat Cumberland.

During their travels across the country the Devil's Clan had kept away from human company as far as possible, but had every now and then come across ragged, desperate Highlanders, all unwilling to join them in their adventure and all attempting to rejoin their families before being caught by the troops. From the lips of these men the reports were all the same. Cumberland had ridden to Inverness and as far as they were concerned, was still there. Alasdair prayed that they had been right, as he sat with the various members of the Devil's Clan amongst the foliage of a clump of trees some two miles from the town.

Tired of going through the endless permutations of plans of attack open to him, he suddenly decided to go ahead with the plan that had been forming in his mind for several days now.

'Well, friends, it is now noon. Shall we make our attack tonight?'

'Yes,' said Hugh Gregor. 'I don't believe our nerves will stand us waiting here for long, and the chances of detection grow stronger by the hour.'

'Well said,' continued Alasdair. 'So we attack tonight. Our major problem is to get someone into the town to spy out Cumberland's house.' He paused for a moment. 'I will go in as soon as it is dark. I have a good friend in town who will know the Duke's whereabouts.'

Jamie scratched his beard for a moment before speaking. 'No. We cannot risk your life just at this moment, for I do not relish the prospect of leading this little expedition. We need you too badly. Let me go in your place. I will find your friend without difficulty, I'm sure.'

'No, no,' chortled Hugh. 'The soldiers will spot your head sticking over the top of the Tolbooth. I swear it. Either myself or Lindsay will have to do it.'

'I am willing,' interjected Lindsay. There was silence for a moment as Alasdair considered their words.

'Why not me?'

Their heads turned in surprise towards Billy who had spoken.

'Now, do not look so surprised. I know the town fairly well for I passed through it several times before they sent me off with Hinchcliffe. I will go dressed in my trousers and boots. I will claim to have been the victim of a rebel attack. The soldiers will look after me as one of their own and will readily give me the information we need. If they will not, then you can give me the name of your friend and I will go and see him. When I have everything I need, I will sneak back here under the pretext of joining my regiment.'

Alasdair nodded enthusiastically. 'Very well, my brave boy. You have talked yourself into a dangerous mission. But, wait, there is a flaw. What if you meet Hinchcliffe?'

'What if I do? He did not see me at the inn, and he does

88

not know where I went after your attack on our camp. I can claim to have been hiding since my narrow escape from your swords on Rannoch. After all, it is partly the truth.'

Alasdair grinned. 'The plan is brilliant, but you will still have to be very careful. Go now, quickly, before you realise what you have agreed to do. I have written down my friend's address here. Tell him I have sent you. He will not turn you away.' The boy quickly removed his plaid and stood in his white trousers and army boots. The clan members rose and patted him on the back, and last of all, Tom embraced him with tears in his eyes.

'Good luck, Billy. May God be with you.'

'Do not worry, Tom. I'll be back before you notice my absence.' With those words the boy slipped through the trees and headed towards Inverness.

'Brave boy,' muttered Alasdair as he and his companions crouched on the ground, but the words were more for re-assurance than anything else. Something was worrying him.

The soldiers spotted the young boy when he was about a hundred yards from them. They raised their rifles out of habit and watched curiously as he stumbled and dragged his feet through the grass towards them. When he was about fifteen yards away he collapsed and they ran towards him. After his face had been lightly slapped several times and some water forced down his throat, his eyes opened and he spoke briefly before appearing to lapse into unconsciousness. Two of the soldiers picked him up by his arms and legs, cursing at his surprising weight, and dragged him off towards the town.

The sun was going down, red and slow, and the day's warmth had already left the air.

Hugh Gregor stirred. 'Damn this waiting. He's been gone for hours. If the soldiers have taken it into their heads to question him closely, they will have all the information they need by now. There's probably a detachment of troops already on its way at this very moment to offer us the hospitality of the army. What do you say we surprise them by taking the initiative? Let's go ahead with our original plan. If we set off now, the town will be in darkness by the time we reach it, and your friend will tell us where Cumberland is situated.'

Alasdair removed from his mouth a piece of salt beef which he had been chewing nervously and tapped it reflectively against the side of his nose.

'Aye, there is much to be said for your idea, Hugh, but there is one important point you have missed. If my friend is not at home, what then? He is a Jacobite and his quarters might have been forcibly seized by the army. It would be a fine thing if we were to knock at his door only for it to be opened by a company of redcoats. I doubt very much whether they would cordially invite us to join their table for a meal.'

Hugh nodded his head slowly in acquiescence. 'Of course, you are right. It is just my nerves. I have never been good at waiting. Pass me some of that beef. The terrible taste might drive such thoughts from my mind.'

The men laughed good-humouredly and Alasdair passed him a piece of the shrivelled, foul-smelling meat. Jamie scratched his beard pensively. 'Did I ever tell you two Gregors about the time when Fingal . . . ' Hugh's voice cut into his narrative.

'My dear Jamie, I should not like to offend you, but after spending some days in your company I would be able to write an epic poem about your great ancestor with nary a pause for thought.'

Jamie returned to scratching his beard, disgruntled at not being able to tell one of his favourite stories. He found it hard to believe that any man could grow bored with tales of heroic deeds and great battles, especially where they concerned Glencoe. But still, the Gregors were a strange people. He had known it since childhood and should not, he reflected, have been surprised by proof of it now.

Dear Glencoe. How he longed to see its gloomy mountains once more, preferably in the company of his uncle, the old devil himself, or better still, with Jeannie. He wondered how she had received his ring and the message he had attached to it. Had she thrown it in anger against the wall, annoyed at his impertinence, or had she laughed when reading the stumbling, clumsy phrases, pitying him for his foolish and unattainable desires? The sooner they had slit Cumberland's fat throat and allowed him to return to her the better he would like it.

Alasdair's thoughts, meanwhile, had turned to his wife, Kathy, for he had been consumed with guilt throughout his journey. Not a moment passed by when he was not assailed with doubts about the course of action he had taken, although he was careful to hide such thoughts from his companions. How could he have been so foolish as to leave her so soon after being reunited? They could now have been happily settled in France, enjoying the patronage of King Louis. He knew that country well, for his father had scraped and saved the money to send him there for his education. How he had loved their fine manners, their great poetry, the richness of their church ceremonial. And Paris! It had been an enchanting place for an eighteen-year old to whom Inverness had formerly seemed a grand city. Those glorious, glittering nights spent dining on exotic food in the company of beautiful, lace-bedecked females. He remembered nights of wild carousing with the help of the finest wine he had ever tasted, and visits to the opera and the theatre where costumes of undreamt luxury and brilliance dazzled the eye wherever he looked. Had it not been for his need of revenge, an ancient lust that coursed through his veins turning logic upside down, he could have been there at the moment with Kathy, her eyes open wide in wonder at his side.

But he was too old to change his nature now, even if such a thing were possible in any event. No matter how strong the allure of handsome clothes, good food and easy living, he would still have chosen to be lying there wrapped in a filthy, stinking plaid, his chin unshaven, chewing unspeakable food and preparing for an evening that would likely prove his last. What, he asked himself, was the point of thinking about it all?

There was no less turmoil in Tom's mind. For a peasant boy whose previous life had been an endless succession of long, exhausting days in the field with his father, the last few months had been an extraordinary experience. First his dreadful time with the army, and now this, in a strange country, sitting with wild-looking warriors who spoke an alien tongue and dressed in unfamiliar clothes, about to take part in an attempt to assassinate the son of his country's King. Such facts were difficult for his young mind to digest, but strangely they did not depress him. Instead he felt his whole body alive with elation, and at the same time, his spirit was soothed by a curious and inexplicable sense of belonging.

A slight breeze had risen and caused the leaves on the tree to rustle, and tugged at the hair projecting from under the warriors' bonnets as they snuggled into their plaids to escape the cold. The shadow of a goshawk passed over their heads, and a stag peered at them through the pine trees before darting away. Alasdair could just make out the hawk through the branches of the trees as it halted suddenly in the middle of its graceful, noiseless flight and fluttered for a moment. Its demoniacal eyes fixed on a spot below and it swooped with breathtaking speed. A tiny screech signalled a successful kill. A good omen, thought Alasdair.

Just as the last light of the day had faded and the men could distinguish each other's faces only with difficulty, there was the sound of a footfall some twenty yards away. Alasdair's hand clasped convulsively at the moss on which he sat and the company held its collective breath. Their hands crept to their dirks, the weapon of the night. Jamie crossed himself in the dark. The footsteps grew louder and louder until Alasdair expected a boot to land at any moment on his clenched fist. Someone breathed heavily just behind him, and a second later, a knee collided with his head and a body toppled over his shoulder. He pounced on it, placing his forearm hard against the intruder's neck. There was a stifled cry followed by choking sounds. Alasdair released the pressure slightly. There was a croak:

'It's me, Billy. Let me go, for the love of God.' Alasdair leapt up and helped the gasping boy to his feet.

'I am sorry, lad, but you were such a long time we feared that the soldiers had discovered our plan. Tell me, is everything arranged?'

'Yes,' rasped the boy. 'I told the soldiers that I was the victim of a vicious attack and they believed me. They took me to the Coffee House at the Cross and fed me and then pointed me in the direction of their camp. I then went to your friend's house. He seemed disturbed to see me at first, but more than pleased to hear that you were alive. He thinks our scheme is madness but will shelter us until it is time to search out Cumberland. He suggests we attack at midnight, just after the sentries have made their rounds.'

'Good, good. This is excellent news.' Alasdair's voice betrayed intense excitement. 'And where is Cumberland?'

'He is lodging in Church Street, opposite St John's Church. Your friend said it was the finest house in town.'

'That will be the Lady Mackintosh's home,' interrupted Jamie. 'I could find it were I blinded in both eyes.'

'He sleeps,' continued Billy, 'on the first floor. It is the second door on the right as you reach the landing. Your friend has drawn a map for us which he is keeping at his house.'

Alasdair cried out in joy and proceeded to dance a short jig before returning to clasp the boy in his arms. 'You have done marvellously well, my young friend. You might turn out to be a true Highlander yet.'

The boy smiled in the darkness.

Hugh Gregor was scarcely less excited than his leader. 'Well, thank the Lord that our waiting is done. Let us leave now, before I go mad.'

'Yes,' said Billy. 'We must get there before nine o'clock, or the sentries will have changed and I told the present ones to expect me back in the company of some Campbells who had been of help to me in my distress and who were camped near the town, frightened to appear lest they be slaughtered in mistake for rebels.'

'By God, but you are a clever boy,' chortled Hugh. 'I promise not to make fun of your strange English ways again.'

'Good. Is everyone ready?' asked Alasdair. 'We shall leave the horses here. If anything goes wrong I do not think we shall have any chance of escape,' he added grimly. 'If anyone wishes to offer any prayers tonight, then this is the time to do it.' The Highlanders bowed their heads and muttered for a while to God, while Tom genuflected and Billy shuffled nervously, impatient to be on his way and preferring to trust in his fellow man rather than any deity.

Presently, their prayers completed, the men silently embraced each other in turn and then made a path through the trees and stole into the night.

CHAPTER TEN

THE WAIT

After skirting the main soldiers' camp situated outside the town and having nearly collided with six naked men hanging by their necks from one sturdy tree – rebels or deserters, they supposed – they at length reached the outskirts of the town. Billy signalled for them to stop and ran in front to speak to the sentries who guarded the main road leading to Inverness.

'We must act like Campbells now,' hissed Alasdair.

'I refuse to crawl on the ground wrapped in a white flag.' Hugh Gregor's sardonic reply caused Jamie to guffaw. Lindsay Hamish poked him in the ribs and Alasdair turned to glare at him.

'Be quiet all of you!'

Billy returned after some minutes of hurried consultation with the guards and winked at Alasdair as he approached. 'It is all right for us to go through as long as I return the tunic they lent me when we leave town. I somehow doubt that we'll have time for that, though.' The boy grinned wryly and led the Highlanders round the sentries and past the low-lying hovels situated at the edge of the town. The men bowed and scraped and grinned foolishly as they passed the sneering sentries in what they, quite wrongly, supposed to be an imitation of general Campbell behaviour.

As they approached the Cross at the centre of town and the houses became larger, they sniffed the air and wondered at the peculiar stench that hung depressingly over the town. The night was almost silent, but every now and then they could hear what sounded like moans and cries of anguish. It sent shivers up and down their spines and Alasdair hoped it might be a trick of the wind.

When they had almost reached their destination, a group of six young officers came reeling out of an alley-way, massively drunk. The Highlanders huddled into the shadows by the side of the road, but were spotted at once by the young blades.

'Good Lord, Courtney, more of the human scum. Hey, you dogs. Come here!' The tallest of the men pointed imperiously at Alasdair who continued to walk forwards, his heart thumping against his ribs. His mouth had dried completely and beads of cold sweat had formed on his brow.

The officer would not be put off, however, and ran over to Alasdair, cheered on by his comrades.

He grabbed hold of his plaid at the neck and wheeled him round so that their faces were almost touching. 'You dare disobey me, you Highland bastard whoreson! Why, I've a good mind to kill you where you stand.' His free hand scrambled to release a pistol from his belt.

Alasdair searched desperately for a way out. He refused to believe that his whole plan would founder on such a stupid incident.

The soldier had located the pistol despite his drunken state, and was drawing it from his belt.

Alasdair blurted a few words in Gaelic.

'What's that, damn you?' The soldier cocked the pistol, and drawing it in front of Alasdair's eyes, pressed it hard against his temple.

The soldier's companions were now shouting excitedly.

'Go on, Winchell, do it.'

'That's the way to treat 'em.'

They began to move threateningly towards the other members of the Devil's Clan who had spreadeagled themselves against the wall of the nearest house. The soldier who held Alasdair by the neck blinked and weaved slightly. 'What's all this damned heathen talk, eh?' He pushed his face even closer to Alasdair, until their noses were no more than an inch apart. 'I want you to understand that I am going to blow your brains out of your thick skull.'

'Please, sir, leave him be, I beg you.'

Billy stepped forward and placed his hand on the soldier's arm. 'These are Campbells. They are on our side.'

'There is no Highlander on my side, I assure you,' the officer shouted, holding the pistol firmly in place.

Billy gripped him harder by the arm. 'Please, sir, but the Duke has asked to see these men tomorrow morning. He wished to thank them for their services at Culloden. I don't think he'd be very pleased to learn that they had been shot by his own men. We all know what a terrible temper he has.'

'Why, you impudent little . . . ' The officer swung his pistol at Billy's head, but the boy weaved under it. The man turned to Alasdair and brought the gun smashing against his cheek. Alasdair gasped in pain and made to grab at his dirk, but caught himself in time. Instead he slumped to the ground uttering a string of Gaelic obscenities which he made to sound like cries for mercy.

The officer looked down at him and aimed a large ball of spit at his head.

'Come on, chaps. We'll deal with these miserable cowards after they've seen that fat little German, Cumberland. Goodnight, scum.' He abruptly turned away and led his companions laughing up the street.

Jamie bent to help Alasdair to his feet. A large, blue-black bruise had begun to spread over his cheek. He breathed harshly through clenched teeth. 'That's another one I promise to take care of,' he growled, staring meaningfully up the street at the back of the receding Englishman. He turned and patted Billy on the back. 'Thank you, laddie, you have saved my life and I am in your debt.' The boy looked abashed and turned away quickly, beckoning for the men to follow him.

Within a few yards they had reached the entrance to a handsome stone house. Alasdair, pausing to look up and down the street, hurried to the door and knocked loudly once, following it by four rapid taps. When he had repeated the formula twice the door flew open to reveal a forbiddingly dark room.

Alasdair hesitated until a voice hissed at him from behind the door. 'Come in, for God's sake. You'll get us all killed unless you hurry.' The men scurried inside and the door slammed shut before the last of them had cleared the threshold.

There followed a terrible, nerve-shattering silence that made Alasdair want to scream. The only light in the room came from a fire which had almost died and Alasdair could discern a shape in front of it. When the shape turned round, it was illuminated by a lit taper which revealed the face of MacLeish, one of Inverness's richest and most respected merchants, an expert on fine wine, a staunch Jacobite and a close friend of Alasdair.

He moved quickly to a table and lit two candles before walking to Alasdair and embracing him in a hug of true affection.

'Well, and what is this crazy scheme I hear tell that you

have concocted? You are all mad, but nevertheless, your lunacy will not have spoiled your appetites. Be seated. I will fetch the food.' So saying, he trotted into the next room.

The men seated themselves in the various chairs placed around the room. MacLeish returned instantly with platters of game meat and steaming mugs filled to the brim with mulled wine. Jamie sipped his drink at once and exclaimed. 'Ah, sir, you must be a merchant, for only some person of that occupation could have gathered so many spices. There must be at least a dozen in this drink.'

MacLeish turned to him and smiled. 'I am indeed a merchant, and there are eight spices to be precise, Mr . . . ?'

'No,' Alasdair hastily interrupted. 'It's best for you that you know as little about us as possible, MacLeish. His first name is Jamie, and this is Hugh, Lindsay, and these two boys are Tom and . . . '

'And Billy. Yes, I have made his acquaintance.'

MacLeish sat down and sipped his wine. 'You realise, do you not, that the town is buzzing with rumours of your little band of avenging angels. They say you have killed over a hundred soldiers and some claim that you have ridden south to kill the King. That is, I think, wishful thinking.' Amid the astonished laughter of the Highlanders he continued: 'They also say that you burn the sign of the cross into the foreheads of your victims. I know that to be true, for I have seen the results of your endeavours on an officer who has recently come to town.'

'Aye, that is true enough,' Jamie concurred, wiping tears of laughter from his cheeks. 'However we have killed nowhere near a hundred men and have, as yet, no intention of killing the King.'

'Only his son,' Alasdair added.

There was a pause in conversation as they ate their food. At length MacLeish turned to Alasdair who was busy wiping the grease from his mouth with the sleeve of his jacket.

'I do not suppose that there is any use in trying to dissuade you from this foolish course of action. You realise, of course, that you will all die.' Alasdair raised his hand as a signal for his friend to stop.

'Our minds are made up. We have not come this far to give up now. I know that our plan must sound crazy to you, but it is just for that very reason it might succeed. Please, do not waste your breath friend. You must know that I am grateful for your concern.'

MacLeish nodded his head and a wry smile played about his lips. 'Very well. I know better than to try to change the mind of a stubborn MacDonald. I have been engaged for too many years in trading with them to believe that possible.'

'Tell me,' asked Hugh. 'What is that filthy smell that hangs over the town and what are the strange moans and cries that fill the streets? I do not mind admitting that they fair turned my stomach.'

A grim look passed over MacLeish's face. 'It soon became obvious that the Toll Booth could harbour no more prisoners after Culloden, so the army has commandeered the largest cellars in town to house rebels and sympathisers. They are packed in so tight that some cannot find space to lie down. They are never allowed out of their holes and fed little food, if any at all. They receive no medical attention, no matter how serious the wounds, and many have already died of festering cuts. There is no provision made for cleanliness, and in some of the cellars, prisoners are sitting up to their waists in their own excrement. Although some of the prisons have doctors in them, they are not allowed to help their sick fellows and are denied the use of their instruments. The tide of the dead swells daily. The soldiers round up beggars and force them to remove the cadavers from the cells and the bodies are piled on carts to be wheeled away to graves outside town.'

His eyes had become bleak during the narrative.

'The trials have begun, and anyone who is tried is executed.'

'We saw the bodies hanging from the trees as we entered the town,' interposed Alasdair.

'Yes, naked no doubt, for what the soldiers do not remove is left for the beggars to take. The beggars fare better than the Jacobites in these dark times . . . The number of prisoners increases so rapidly despite the rate of death that I fear they will soon be transported to ships in the Firth, and that could prove an even worse fate for them.'

'How do you know all this?' asked Hugh.

'I went to visit a friend in prison. They would not let me speak to him until I had bribed the guard. The cellar was almost completely dark and so devoid of air that I feared I would collapse as soon as I had entered. By the light of the torches I could make out dead bodies and others so close to death that the difference seemed scarcely to matter. Their ragged clothes were filthy and they lay in their own waste. The smell was indescribable. Many were half-starved and shook

98

with fever, and some lay with great, gaping wounds in their arms and legs. Most were covered in sores that on some of them, threatened to engulf their whole body. My friend, another merchant, was imprisoned for a drunken toast to Prince Charlie in the Coffee House. It was a foolish deed and one that he has subsequently paid for with his life. The food I took to him was soon confiscated by the guards. So the smell that hangs over the town is one of diseased and rotting corpses, and would you believe that amidst all this vile torture Cumberland has ordered the streets to be cleaned?'

A mixture of emotions had flashed across the faces of the listening men – horror, disgust, disbelief and sadness – but now they all sat with their jaws set in an attitude of grim determination.

Alasdair was the first to speak. 'And how have you saved yourself from such a fate, MacLeish?'

'I am ashamed to admit that I have bought my freedom with heavy bribes paid to various officers and sentries, and gifts of brandy and claret. But my money is fast running out. I have spent the rest in attempting to secure relief for some of the prisoners – mainly food and medical supplies. As my life will not be worth a tinker's curse when I can no longer pay, I am off to France on one of my boats tomorrow. I feel it is an act of cowardice, but having seen the prisons, I have no desire to enjoy such accommodation.'

'You have been mighty brave, my friend,' Alasdair assured him, 'and I am sorry to have placed you in further danger.'

'Think nothing of it. If your scheme succeeds, then I shall be the happiest man in Scotland. Cumberland is a pig that deserves sticking. By the way, your task will no doubt be made much easier by the fact that the town is out of bounds to all common soldiers except the sentries and the hourly patrols. Come, let me fill your glasses and then I will show you the map I have made of Cumberland's quarters.' He returned after a few moments with more drinks and a folded piece of paper which he spread on the table and beckoned his visitors to stand around him.

'Here is Church Street and here is St John's Chapel. The house is directly opposite the church. Here is a small wynde leading up the side of the house. There is a door here which leads directly up to the first floor. Cumberland's bedroom is the second door on the right.'

'And are there any guards?' asked Jamie.

99

'No, or at least, I have not heard of any. Cumberland is so sure of his safety that he seems willing to do without them. He has created such a reign of fear in Inverness that until now he has been proved correct.'

Each of the Highlanders studied the map in turn and nodded when satisfied that they had memorised its contents. 'Now,' continued MacLeish, 'the patrol that goes past Cumberland's house also comes past here, usually at midnight, and walks away in the opposite direction. You will have to leave as soon as it has passed. One of the maids in the house tells me that the Duke often sits at his desk writing between the hours of midnight and one o'clock – his memoirs no doubt. The desk is directly in front of you as you enter the room. I suggest that whichever of you is most accurate throws a dirk into his back.'

Alasdair dismissed the idea. 'No, I want to see the fear on his face and I want him to know why he is being executed.'

MacLeish looked thoughtful. 'You do realise, I suppose, that his death will create more bloodshed in these parts?'

'I have thought long and hard on that point, I assure you. It is not easy to carry the burden of yet more of my countrymen's deaths on my shoulders, but it looks as if the English are determined to erase our very memory from these Highlands. If we are doomed, then we are doomed. If we are successful in our attempt then we might very well find support for our cause, so at least we will die fighting. There is nothing so sad as being murdered in one's bed. That is a lesson the Campbells taught us very well but fifty years ago.'

MacLeish nodded. He was sorry for having brought up the argument in the first place, for Alasdair's thoughts mirrored his own. Perhaps he would not catch the boat to France after all. He had, he felt, been a merchant too long and making money would seem a foolish occupation in the light of the events following Culloden. He would wait until midnight and then announce that he was going with them. His clothes, worn in the English style, would make an excellent cover for their journey across town. Their plan decided, the men resumed their seats and sat in thoughtful silence, with MacLeish intoning the time every quarter of an hour.

As the hands of the clock crept round to a quarter of an hour before midnight, Billy became restless.

'Would you like me to go out and scout the streets until we leave?'

'No, boy,' Alasdair shook his head. 'We cannot afford any upsets now. There are only fifteen minutes to go. Sit still.'

MacLeish rose from his seat.

'I had better tell you now that I intend to leave with you.' The assembled company gasped at his revelation. Hugh Gregor was the first to speak. 'But pardon me, sir, you are a merchant. Look at yourself, dressed in fine clothes that cover your belly, and with your soft merchant's hands. You have already done more than enough. I fear you will be of precious little use to us in a fight. Stay man, and sail for France. You can help our cause by persuading King Louis to send us fresh troops.'

MacLeish's eyes flashed angrily. 'I have not always been a merchant, sir. I was very much like yourself until the winter that my family died of starvation. I decided to renounce poverty then and have become rich in my trade, but never again as happy as I was back in my own hills.' His eyes clouded as memories flooded into his mind.

'But that,' Hugh continued, 'must have been many years ago. How do you intend to fight now? By standing and throwing money at the enemy, I suppose.' MacLeish, enraged by Hugh's sarcasm, drew a dagger concealed under his black coat and leapt at his tormentor. Hugh rolled from his seat just in time, for the dirk thudded into the chair a second after he had vacated it. Alasdair and Jamie leapt at MacLeish and pinned his arms to the ground.

'You'll spoil everything, damn you,' Alasdair shouted into his face. 'We are minutes away from our goal, and now you decide to go crazy. What has come over you? Listen to Hugh!'

Hugh got to his feet, brushed the dust from his plaid and walked towards his assailant, hand outstretched in friendship. 'Come friend, I only goaded you for your own sake. I do not doubt your bravery, and have no wish to quarrel with you . . . especially if it is likely to lead to my death.'

MacLeish grinned suddenly, and shrugging off the hands that grasped his arms, rose to his feet and proffered his hand to Hugh. 'I am very sorry. You annoyed me only because you were correct. I realise that I could be of little use to you in a fight. I shall take your advice and leave for France tomorrow as I originally intended. I apologise to you all for . . . '

Alasdair shushed him to be quiet and the room became silent. In the distance they could hear the rhythmic tramp of boots. MacLeish glanced at his watch. One minute to midnight. The soldiers approached closer until they were directly outside MacLeish's door . . . and then they stopped. All breathing appeared to cease in the room, and then the church bell began tolling midnight. The soldiers marched on. MacLeish ran to the door and whispered for Alasdair to snuff out the candles. He opened the door and swiftly poked his head around its side, looking hurriedly up and down the street. He beckoned the Highlanders and clapped each one of them on the back as they exited into the stench-filled night air. Alasdair was the last. He turned to MacLeish before he left and hugged him before joining his comrades.

As soon as they had gone MacLeish closed the door and leant against it, breathing heavily in the darkness.

CHAPTER ELEVEN

THE ASSASSINATION

Alasdair found his followers waiting for him outside, huddled against the wall of the house. He glanced quickly up the street and plunged into the alley that ran down the side of MacLeish's house leading to Church Street. He paused at the end of the alley and signalled for his companions to stop, and satisfied that the road was empty, stepped out from the shadows.

'And who the devil are you?' Alasdair gaped in astonishment. A wizened old man dressed entirely in black cloth stared up at him.

'I . . . I am a special Campbell guard. I am patrolling this street to ensure the Duke's safety. There is no need for you to be alarmed.'

The old man sniffed at the explanation and walked towards the door of the house next to the alley and searched in his pockets for a key. 'Well, I suppose I should be grateful for all this protection, but I must admit I find it a damned unsettling nuisance. Good-night to you, sir.' He opened the door, walked in and slammed it angrily.

Alasdair whistled softly, relieved that his companions had not followed him into the street at once.

'And you are a damned unsettling nuisance,' Hugh Gregor whispered in imitation of the old man as he crept up behind Alasdair. When they had all gathered together, Alasdair bade them walk slowly down the street. St John's Chapel was now in view across the road and there were only about a hundred yards between them and Cumberland's house which was directly opposite the church.

The street was dark and deserted and Alasdair controlled an impulse to burst from the shadows and race down it. Instead, they continued to crawl past the walls of the stone houses that separated them from their quarry. Yard by yard, foot by foot, stone by stone, they inched nearer the house, until after what seemed like an eternity, they reached the edge of the neighbouring building.

Alasdair turned to Hugh. 'Is everyone all right?'

'I'll see.' Hugh turned to Jamie, who spoke to Lindsay, who turned to Tom, who turned to find only darkness behind him.

'Billy?' He stretched his hand out into the gloom but met only mortar and stone. 'Billy?' he cooed, slightly louder this time.

'Shut up, boy, you'll get us all killed,' hissed Alasdair.

Tom trotted up the line of men until he had reached Alasdair. 'He's gone.'

'Who's gone?'

'Billy. I can't see any sign of him. He's disappeared.' Alasdair's jaws clenched. 'Have you heard or seen anything unusual since we left MacLeish's house?'

Tom thought hard. 'No, not a thing. I looked back not a minute ago and he was still there. Perhaps he just became frightened.'

'Perhaps. Anyway, we cannot worry about him now. Gather round, everyone.' Just as the Highlanders began to move, the door to Cumberland's house opened and two officers stepped out on to the street. The door closed behind them and, deep in conversation, they strolled up the road towards the Devil's Clan.

'You know, I feel that we're in danger of going too far with these Highlanders.'

'Nonsense, sir. Cumberland is right. They are animals, no more and no less, and deserve to be treated accordingly.'

'No, no,' the first soldier shook his head in violent disagreement. 'If you attempt to exterminate them we will earn the undying hatred of any that survive. Can you imagine the danger of another insurrection with the sole purpose of taking revenge upon the English people. Why, it would be unspeakable. We should treat them with kindness and thereby prevent another outbreak of this kind. Anyway, I do not relish the prospect of being loathed in perpetuity by succeeding generations of Scotsmen.' The men were within spitting distance now, and Jamie squeezed against the wall with all his might in an attempt to hide his great bulk. The first soldier was within a step of him, and as the man gesticulated to emphasise a point he was making, his elbow struck Jamie's stomach. Astonishingly the speaker did not notice the contact and the two men carried blandly on until they were out of sight.

'Thank God,' muttered Jamie. 'I should not have enjoyed

104

killing him after his arguments on our behalf.'

'Come, let us to our work.' hissed Alasdair. The five men tiptoed across the front of Cumberland's house until they had reached the alley beyond, the 'wynde' that MacLeish had referred to. They held a speedy conference just within its protective darkness. 'Tom, you will stay here, signal if soldiers come in force.' The rest of the group scuttled down the alley until they had reached the door marked on MacLeish's map.

Lindsay brought out a metal hoop with five keys on it holding it tight in case it made a noise. 'Go to it, Lindsay. MacLeish promised us that those keys would open any lock in Inverness. Let's prove him right,' whispered Alasdair. Lindsay, having selected a key, felt for the keyhole. When he attempted to insert it, the door swung slowly open, creaking slightly.

'Good God,' Alasdair was shocked. 'Well, this is what I call luck. Now, Hugh, you come with me . . . Jamie and Lindsay, you will stay here. If you hear a disturbance above, then run for your lives, for ours will surely be lost no matter what you do.' He turned to Jamie. 'I am sorry you are not coming with me, old friend, but you really are too big. God knows what noise you might make getting up those stairs.'

'I understand, friend. I wish you good luck.' Alasdair turned quickly away and entered the black doorway, his foot searching for the first step of the staircase which would lead them to Cumberland. His toe tapped against it and he began to climb in the pitch black. His back slid up the wall on his lefthand side and one of his hands grasped the banister on the right, while Hugh Gregor clung to his kilt for guidance, like a young child following its mother.

When they had ascended fifteen steps, Alasdair could discern a light ahead of him which appeared to be emanating from the bottom of a door near the top of the stairs. All moisture disappeared from his mouth as he tried to swallow, and his heart pumped at a furious pace. The last few steps were agonisingly slow, but eventually they reached the landing. They could now see that the light was indeed coming from the bottom of a door, and if MacLeish's information was correct, it was coming from Cumberland's room. Alasdair prayed that he might be writing at his desk as his maid had suggested he would.

Both men removed their dirks and pistols and inched their way towards the door. Alasdair's hand moved towards the door knob. It made no sound as it moved, but the door creaked slightly as it swung open. They stepped inside the room. The walls were hung with beautiful blue and gold tapestries and the room contained a comfortable-looking four-poster bed.

Seated directly in front of them was a man, dressed in a white sleeping gown, hunched over some papers on a desk, apparently engrossed in his work. Alasdair felt dizzy with a mixture of fear and elation. He tried to speak, but at first no sound issued from his throat. He tried again.

'Cumberland, it is time for you to say your prayers.'

'No, Mr MacDonald, it is undoubtedly time for you to say yours.'

The tapestries were flung aside and out stepped six soldiers armed with pistols.

'Stand back!' cried Alasdair, 'or I kill the Duke.'

The man at the desk spoke again. 'You would find that rather difficult, my dear MacDonald.' The figure rose and turned slowly to face them. Alasdair and Hugh gasped in astonishment. From underneath the sleeping cap, Hinchcliffe's deformed face grinned wickedly up at them.

Alasdair, completely stunned, allowed his pistol to drop from his hand. It clattered noisily on the wooden floorboards of the room. Hugh Gregor, his jaw slack with surprise, allowed his arm to fall to his side. A soldier stepped forward to retrieve Alasdair's fallen gun and to remove Hugh's pistol from his hand, and moved back into line with his comrades.

Hinchcliffe arose slowly from his seat. A black patch covered his mutilated eye, and the night-cap was pulled down on one side to hide what was left of his ear. He walked over to Alasdair, his jaws working. When he reached the Highlander he pursed his lips and spat into his face. The ball of liquid hit Alasdair on the forehead and trickled over his eyelid and on to his cheek. His fists clenched involuntarily, but he allowed no sign of emotion to show on his face.

'Come, Mr MacDonald, have you lost your pride?' Hinchcliffe spoke through clamped teeth, and his upper lip flared on one side. 'Perhaps this will alter your expression.' He tore off the eyepatch and Alasdair could not help gasping in horror at the sight. Some of the white of the eye was still visible, but for the most part it was a horrible mass of scars and caked blood. A surgeon had made some clumsy attempts to stitch the wound and pieces of catgut stuck out of the mess at several points.

'Yes, MacDonald, you may well blanch at the sight. It is

not a pleasing prospect, is it?' He cocked his head to one side, his good eye still fixed on Alasdair. 'Eh, do you refuse to answer me? IS THIS A PLEASANT SIGHT?' The scream echoed in the small room.

Hugh Gregor turned his head to look at Hinchcliffe.

'No, my dear Captain, I am in full agreement with you. Now, would you please cover it up as we have just eaten our dinner. You are not aiding my digestion.'

Hinchcliffe leapt at him and brought his clenched fist smashing across his face, knocking Hugh to his knees.

'That is the last time you'll laugh at me, you villainous pig. You will enjoy a traitor's death tomorrow. They will hang you slowly, and while you strangle to death and your face turns blue and your tongue pops out of your head, they'll slit your stomach, pull out your guts and hold them up in front of your eyes. They will be the last thing you see. I doubt whether that will aid your digestion either.' He was breathing heavily and a rictus grin of loathing distorted his face. 'But that's not all. The Duke has asked me to interrogate you before your death. He believes you hold secret information from King Louis. In fact he believes that it was that damned Frenchie that sent you to kill him.'

'But that is a lie!' Alasdair had spoken for the first time since being disarmed.

'But, don't you see, my dear old friend, that your refusal to admit the fact makes interrogation necessary.' Hinchcliffe giggled insanely. 'I can assure you that it will last all night.' His eye gleamed wickedly. 'I believe we have unfinished business to attend to. You look surprised. Do you not remember our little conversation on Rannoch Moor, the one that Mr Gregor here interrupted so rudely? Well we now have a chance to resume where we were forced to leave off, if you get my meaning.'

Hugh Gregor looked up, his face masked in disbelief.

'You surely cannot mean that you intend . . . ?' The question was left hanging in the air, for Alasdair had bolted for the door. Three soldiers were on him immediately and his struggles ceased after a few moments. The three other redcoats moved in on Hugh and dragged him to his feet.

'Where are you taking us?' asked Alasdair.

'To meet the Duke who is at this moment enjoying a quiet meal at the Coffee House in the Cross. He is probably having a pleasant conversation with one of your friends, Mr MacLeish.

Yes, think of it, you have been sitting all evening just yards away from your quarry. Ironic, I think you'll agree.'

Alasdair had gasped at the mention of his friend's name.

'You cannot mean that MacLeish has betrayed us?'

'No, no, quite the contrary. He is due to enjoy your fate tomorrow or should I say,' he removed a gold timepiece from the pocket of his night shirt, 'today, for we have certainly passed the hour of midnight. Your signal, I believe, for starting this foolish expedition.' Alasdair was shocked afresh. 'And who told you all this? Who has betrayed us?'

Hinchcliffe smiled wryly. 'Can you not guess?'

Then it dawned on Alasdair.

Billy! He must have gone straight to Hinchcliffe on reaching the town before he had even met MacLeish, and must then have returned to give the Captain full details of their plan. Letting them get so far had merely been a sadistic trick of Hinchcliffe's. Alasdair felt sick to his stomach as he thought of the days they had spent with the youngster, teaching him Highland ways, accepting him into their every confidence, sharing their food with him. He swore that he would never trust an Englishman again. Perhaps even Tom had been involved in the scheme. The thought saddened him, for he had conceived a great affection for the boy.

'Come, MacDonald, you are not slow-witted, whatever else you are,' Hinchcliffe prodded.

Alasdair remained silent. Every moment that he delayed Hinchcliffe, better was the chance that Jamie might escape . . . if the big ox had taken his advice seriously.

'Billy, damn you,' Hinchcliffe shouted. 'Your charming little friend. No sooner had he reached the town than he ran to me with weird and wonderful tales. The English have made a fool out of you, you poor wretch.'

Heavy boots tramped up the stairs and a soldier burst into the room. 'Captain, we have captured both of them. The big one put up quite a struggle and the other has stabbed one of my men.'

'Both of them? Where is the boy?'

'Do not worry, sir, he told us that he was working under your directions and that he was ordered to return to camp as soon as we came.'

Hinchcliffe screamed in rage. 'You fool! There won't be a shred of skin on your back after you've paid for this. I told you to get the boy. He is no more in my employ than these savages.' He pointed at the two Highlanders. He turned to Alasdair. 'Don't smirk, MacDonald, we'll get the young bastard. I'll tear his yellow liver out and smear it across his face. All right men, take them downstairs.'

The soldiers pocketed their pistols and took the rifles from their shoulders before pushing the prisoners down the narrow stairs. At the end of the alley in the street, stood Jamie and Lindsay, dejected and ashamed, also held prisoner.

'I am sorry Alasdair, but we didn't see them . . . ' Jamie was silenced with the thump of a rifle butt across his head.

'Be quiet all of you!' Hinchcliffe strutted to the front of the group and led the way back to the Cross. There were ten soldiers in all, for two of them had been wounded in apprehending Jamie and Lindsay and had left to seek medical attention. One of the redcoats walked behind Hinchcliffe, with three of his companions behind him followed by Lindsay and Alasdair who in turn had three rifles pointed at their backs. Bringing up their rear were the last three soldiers who concentrated on Alasdair and Hugh.

An old Highland woman, wrapped in a tartan shawl, stumbled out of one of the many alleys leading off the road and crashed into Hinchcliffe. The captain raised his hand to strike at her, but received a butt in the stomach from her head. The four soldiers behind jumped forward to his aid. A shot rang out and one of the redcoats fell to his knees, clutching at his heart. Another shot came and then another and two more soldiers toppled forward, while the woman leapt on to the last redcoat's back and grasped him round the throat. As soon as the first shot had rung out, the Highlanders had acted, turning with immense speed upon their captors.

Only Lindsay had acted too slowly, for when he turned, the soldier immediately behind him fired straight into his stomach and he had fallen to the ground, hands clasped to his belly. With terrifying ferocity the other Highlanders had set to work, punching, kicking and biting, elated by the turn of events. Alasdair had torn the rifle from the hands of the nearest redcoat and stabbed him in the neck with a vicious thrust while Jamie had hoisted one of them into the air, before dashing his head against the ground. Hugh, snarling like a wild animal had knocked his opponent senseless with brutal blows from the sides of his two hands.

At length all the soldiers had been taken care of and Alasdair looked around to see two figures chasing up the road, too far away to be followed or identified. Meanwhile Hugh busied himself by skipping between the soldiers, burying a dagger in their hearts to make sure that they were dead. He soon came to the old woman, who was lying stunned under the body of the redcoat whose neck she had broken. Hugh shifted the dead man and helped the woman to her feet. Slowly, she removed her shawl. Tom's face smiled at them from under the tartan cloth and Alasdair's heart leaped to see the boy whom he had so recently doubted. He walked over to him and hugged his head against his breast, overcome with emotion.

The sound of hurrying footsteps broke into his thoughts. He looked up to see MacLeish, a rifle still in his hand.

'I'm sorry, Alasdair,' he said, gasping for air. 'I have been chasing that officer, but he runs like a hare, damn him, and I am an old, soft merchant.'

He glanced meaningfully at Hugh, who blushed with embarrassment. 'If I ever call you that again, MacLeish, you have permission to shoot me.'

'If you ever do, I'll do it without your permission, but come on, we can't hang around here. The soldiers will be along shortly.' So saying, he took to his heels and set off at a great pace up the road. As they ran, they noticed lights going on in all the houses as candles were lit, doors were being opened and heads were poking out from windows.

The Highlanders ran until their lungs had emptied of air, and then ran some more in a desperate attempt to keep up with MacLeish who had dived unexpectedly into an alley which, the Highlanders could see as they rounded the corner, led into a small close. Four horses stood saddled in the square. With whoops of joy the Highlanders leapt on to them, while Hugh bent to help Tom on to his horse. They wheeled the animals round and tore up the alley and on to the road once more. No sooner had they reached it than at least two dozen soldiers on horseback hove into view led by Hinchcliffe, screaming at the top of his voice and firing pistol shots. The Highlanders dug their heels in and rode as they had never ridden before, the dirt of the road rising in thick clouds to choke their pursuers.

As they approached the squalid buildings at the end of the street a group of amazed sentries came out of the shadows and stood gaping at them. Just as they raised their rifles to fire, Hugh Gregor unsheathed his sword, and taking care not to unseat Tom, bent down and slit one of the soldier's throats as

110

he raced past. 'That is for Lindsay,' he screamed as the four horses galloped furiously past the soldiers' camp and into the darkness.

Behind them the riders came to a halt. Hinchcliffe raced on alone for a few hundred yards before he realised that no one was following him. He stopped quickly, not relishing the idea of coming upon the Highlanders without support, and rode back to the troops in a state of fury. When he reached their captain he began yelling.

'What in hell's name are you doing, sir? I'll have you shot for cowardice. This will be the end of your career.' The soldiers began sniggering at his unseemly conduct, but their commander turned in his saddle and ordered them to be quiet before returning to face Hinchcliffe.

'Sir, you are making a fool of yourself. As we are both of the rank of captain, I fail to see how you intend to finish my career.'

'I'll tell Cumberland, damn you. I shouldn't imagine he'll be too pleased to hear of your behaviour.'

The officer smiled to himself. 'And I shouldn't imagine he'll be too pleased to hear about your lack of success this evening.' Hinchcliffe flushed with rage and the Captain continued hurriedly. 'Once those scoundrels had reached the outskirts of the town, they were beyond our reach. They will know the surrounding countryside too well to allow us to catch them on such a dark night. Look up there,' he glanced at the sky. 'There is no moon. I have no intention of making our horses lame by riding them over rough terrain in the pitch darkness. Let us be rational about it.'

'Damn your rationality, sir,' cried Hinchcliffe. 'In fact, damn you and damn all of you.' His horse reared into the air and he plunged back down the road towards town followed by the mocking laughter of the troopers.

Jamie's horse buckled under him and he shot forward over its neck. As he lay groaning, the others halted and rode back to help. It was time that they stopped, reflected MacLeish, for they had ridden for at least seven miles and there was no danger that the cavalrymen would have followed them successfully across such treacherous ground on such a black night. Jamie's yell had brought him up short, and by the time he had ridden back the huge man had been helped to his feet and stood with

111

his hands clutching his temples, trying to ease the pain from his head. MacLeish walked over to Jamie's horse which lay panting on its side, and felt over its legs for signs of fracture. Luckily, the animal had escaped unharmed. It had obviously just been exhausted from carrying such a heavy weight. MacLeish patted the animal on the muzzle and searched his pocket for a sweet to give it.

Alasdair, having satisfied himself as to Jamie's safety strolled over to MacLeish. 'Man, you are an old devil. Did I not tell you to stay at home minding your money.'

MacLeish laughed. 'I have so little of it left that it took me but a few moments and then I thought of you and of the boy you sent to me. I did not much like the look of him and he seemed too eager to set a plan at once. We have all learned to be suspicious during the past weeks. There have been enough Highland traitors to our cause, let alone English ones. He had slit eyes and looked like a young pig and that is just what he turned out to be.'

'When did you leave your house?'

'Minutes after you. I began thinking about the boy and then I had such a feeling of impending doom that I had to follow you. No sooner had I reached the alley by the side of the house than soldiers marched past me and went straight to my door which they broke through without so much as a knock. I ran to Church Street and was near the end of the alley which goes by the house next to Lady Mackintosh's establishment when young Tom ran smack into me. He began yelling and punching me before realising who he had collided with. We crept to the end of the alley and you appeared with your escort. I wrapped Tom's plaid over his head to make him look like an old washerwoman and cocked my pistol and rifle and the rest you know.'

Alasdair shook his head in wonder. 'You really are the most remarkable man I have ever met. You look like a meek, church-going banker and here you are behaving like a warrior from legend. It is enough to confuse a man.'

MacLeish grinned. 'As long as it's enough to confuse the English then I'm more than happy.'

Hugh, Jamie and Tom gathered around the two men. Alasdair rose and faced Hugh. 'My friend, I cannot say how sorry I am for what happened to Lindsay. I know that he was your greatest friend.'

Alasdair could not see his face in the darkness but heard

him snuffling and guessed that he had been crying. 'Thank you, Alasdair. It is not easy for me to lose him. We have been inseparable for years. I know that he seemed a quiet mouse of a man to others, but he was a lion underneath. I have seen him do things that you would not believe. Still, if he had to die, then this was the best way.'

Alasdair searched for the right words. 'I suppose I did not hear him speak more than a hundred words all the hours that we were together, but I had grown to like and respect him. We are all very sorry.' He was silent for a moment. 'He died a brave man.'

Hugh broke into painful sobs and walked away, grief wringing his heart. Alasdair let him go.

'Where are we, MacLeish?' he called to his companion.

'Smell the air, Alasdair. Can you not tell?'

Alasdair sniffed. 'We are near a loch, but which one?'

'Oh, you'll not have heard of it. 'Tis but a small thing, but the water is best in these parts. Let's take our horses to the water's edge and then get some sleep. The soldiers will not be on our tail till morning.'

As he turned towards his horse something crashed into Alasdair's head and his mind went as blank as the night sky.

CHAPTER TWELVE

THE JOURNEY

Cumberland sat at the central table in the coffee house, his lips pursed in displeasure. Standing across the table from him was Hinchcliffe, a look of deep embarrassment on that part of his face which was visible. Cumberland had ordered him to cover his wounds – 'They are most displeasing to me, sir' – and the Captain now stood with a handkerchief draped ludicrously over his head to mask his damaged ear and eye. Hinchcliffe noted wryly that the same request had not been made at their first meeting.

The Duke had listened patiently to Hinchcliffe's account of the night's proceedings and was most put out. He had been waiting for the better part of the evening in the dirty, stinking room that served as the town's main meeting place, and his wait had been in almost complete darkness lest his presence be detected. He had been quite jolly in conversation with some of his officers who had been brought in for the entertainment, and had broken open a bottle of his favourite brandy. And now his little diversion had been ruined. Hinchcliffe had promised him faithfully that at thirty minutes after midnight the door would open to reveal a team of would-be assassins, and the Duke had been looking forward to the prospect of meeting these impudent lunatics face to face.

Instead, Hinchcliffe had burst through the door a full quarter of an hour late, alone, babbling excuses before he had even explained what he was excusing himself for. And the man looked so awful. Cumberland was not one to turn away from the sight of wounds. Many of his soldiers were scarred beyond recognition, and he had seen quite a few arms and legs sawn off crudely in field hospitals during his brief career. But Hinchcliffe was an officer and there was something offensive about a mutilated officer, as if his scars bore mute testimony to his incompetence. The fact that this man's wounds had not even been received in battle made them almost obscene in the eyes of the commander of the King's army.

When the night's events had been revealed in all their sordid detail, Cumberland had been furious and his anger had abated not at all. Two bright red marks had spread across his cheeks, partly through the quantity of alcohol he had consumed and partly through the intense emotion that Hinchcliffe's narrative had caused in him.

'Sir,' he said after a long pause. 'You have been made to look extremely foolish and as a representative of our Majesty's army, you have made every soldier in that army look foolish, to mention nothing of myself and my officers.' Cumberland snorted loudly, causing Hinchcliffe to flinch, and removed a handkerchief from his cuff to blow his nose. The trumpeting sound he produced caused a suppressed giggle from the officers ranged behind him.

'I was grateful to you for bringing me news of his attempt on my life, for who can tell, it might have proved successful had the scheme remained undetected. And for that I am still thankful to you. Indeed, it is for that reason alone that I have decided not to reduce your rank.' Hinchcliffe breathed an almost audible sigh of relief. 'But to have the villains in the palm of your hand, and guarded by ten of my soldiers, and to let them escape, that is quite unforgivable.'

'But, sir, they . . .'

'SILENCE!' Cumberland lumbered to his feet and leant across the table. 'If you dare have the impertinence to interrupt me again I'll have you court-martialled. This is not a dialogue, damn you.' The Duke, his face suffused with pink, slumped back into his seat. He glared at Hinchcliffe who had begun to shake visibly. 'I shall not give you another post of honour in my army until you have brought me the head of their leader, this Alasdair MacDonald, and some definite proof that it is his head. You have a sly look about you that would make me doubt your word alone. Meanwhile, you retain the rank of captain and you are officially transferred to the Intelligence Service. You may dress as you please. I will give you a letter signed by me which should prove of help.' He snapped his fingers and pen and ink and paper were hastily provided by one of the officers standing behind him. He scribbled for a few moments, shook salt on the paper, blew it off and threw the letter back across the desk.

'Do not fail me this time, Captain, or I will break you. If anything transpires in the near future, and I hope for your sake that it does, I am leaving for Fort Augustus. Bring me the man, or his head, there and you will have gone some considerable way towards redeeming yourself in my eyes. Now leave us.'

Hinchcliffe turned instantly and suppressed a strong desire to sprint away. Instead he walked in as dignified a fashion as he could manage while the laughter of the officers in the room followed him every step of the way. Each time he had crossed swords with Alasdair MacDonald, his reward had been derision. His jaws set determinedly.

When he had shut the door of the coffee house securely behind him, he walked for a few yards and leant, exhausted, against the nearest door. His body was soaked in sweat. He realised with a start that he was leaning on the door of Mac-Leish's house. Could that have been the strange man who had pursued him so ferociously after the ambush in George Street? He had certainly not been in his house when the troops had called for him. If he had indeed joined MacDonald, then that was just another score for Hinchcliffe to settle.

Alasdair's head was throbbing when he woke up. From the lack of wind he guessed that he was inside a building of sorts. Loud snores told him that he was not alone.

He opened his eyes slowly. He was lying in a cramped hut. The other members of the Devil's Clan were dotted around the floor. There had been a fire during the night, for he could still smell the smoke, but it had gone out, and despite the fact that they had moved into May, the hut was intensely cold. From this fact he surmised that it was early morning. He crept across the floor towards the entrance of the hovel, careful not to wake his companions. As he crawled he tried to recall what had happened. He remembered a shadow brushing past him in the night, a crack on his head, and then no more. He felt the top of his skull gingerly. There was a huge bump where he had been hit.

He had reached the entrance to the hut and poked his head slowly outside. He was staring into the barrel of a flintlock rifle. A fierce Highlander with bushy eyebrows and piercing black eyes was holding the gun. Alasdair saw with relief that he was wearing the white cockade of the Jacobites in his bonnet. He decided to speak.

'Good morning to you, friend.'

The Highlander's eyes narrowed in suspicion.

'I should like to know what gives you the right to call me friend, Campbell. And do not move or I will blow away your head.'

Alasdair was astonished.

'All right, get up now, but slowly.' The Highlander moved backwards a few paces and allowed Alasdair to stand, but kept the gun pointing straight at his head.

Alasdair began talking hurriedly. 'Look, now, I call you friend because you wear the white in your bonnet. And how you ever got the crazy idea that I was a Campbell, I shall never know.'

'Who are you, then?'

'I am Alasdair MacDonald of Glencoe.'

'And who is your chief?'

'McIan, of course. For God's sake man, this is a child's game we are playing.'

The Highlander seemed confused. 'Step over to that hut.' He beckoned with his rifle to a hut on the other side of the small village. When they had reached it, the Highlander leant down and knocked at the rickety wooden door. 'They are awake.'

The door was opened by a man so small he was almost dwarf-like. His short bow-legs supported the heavy body of a man twice his height, and his head was in proportion to his body. He would have been comical had it not been for the fierceness of his expression. He spat on the ground. 'So, you are awake, you Campbell bastard.'

'He says he is not a Campbell, father.'

The old man laughed. 'Not a Campbell?'

He leapt at Alasdair and knocked him to the ground. The old man soon had him pinned securely to the ground, a huge hairy forearm pressing against his windpipe.

'Do not lie to me, you who learnt deceit at your mother's breast.' The old man rose abruptly and turned to his son. 'Shoot him first. Do it now. That should awaken the others.'

Alasdair stared at the gun which was once again pointing at his head. He was too aghast to speak. He could think of nothing to say. The irony of the situation was so terrible that he could not believe that it was happening. The boy licked his lips and moved his head so that his right eye stared along the sights of his barrel.

'Are you mad?' The boy turned to find Jamie and Hugh standing outside their hut. 'That man has just tried to assassinate the Duke of Cumberland. What do you think you are doing?' The Highlander became confused once more.

His father came back out of his hut, clutching another rifle.

He shouted across to Jamie. 'Keep your slippery tongue to yourself, Campbell.'

It was Jamie's turn to be amazed.

'Campbell? I am no Campbell. I'm from Glencoe.'

The old man cackled sarcastically. 'I suppose your family left you behind after the Massacre.'

'What makes you think I am a Campbell, you old madman?'

Tom and MacLeish stumbled out of the hut, awakened by the noise.

The old man pointed triumphantly at them.

'They do, my friend. I heard them talking last night before we attacked. The boy is a Sassenach, and him,' – he pointed to MacLeish – 'look at him! A damned merchant from Inverness, if I'm not much mistaken and they are all Englishmen under the surface. I do not know what kind of mission you are on, but it is not for the good of King James, I'll warrant.'

Alasdair struggled to his feet and found his tongue.

'Listen to me, old man, before you make a terrible mistake. That man is an Inverness merchant, true enough, but he's as much a Highlander as you are and the proudest Jacobite in Inverness. He risked his life last night to save us from Cumberland's soldiers. The boy is an Englishman, aye, and a soldier, but he has deserted because of their cruelty to him and he is now a believer in our cause. He's had many a chance to escape from us, but has remained even at moments of great danger. I am from Glencoe as is that great ox of a man standing there.' He pointed at Jamie. 'He is Jamie McIan, nephew to old McIan. The other is Hugh Gregor from Rannoch. We three fought at Culloden and fought hard. The least you could do is listen to our story.'

The old man was thoughtful for a moment. Something about Alasdair's voice, a certain unmistakable sincerity, had touched him and he nodded his head slowly, agreeing to the suggestion.

'Very well, gather together here.' He pointed to a spot some ten yards from him. When the Clan had moved to the place indicated, the old man bade them sit.

'Tell your stories, but make them brief and make them convincing. I warn you, I am a very suspicious old man.'

Alasdair began with his own escape from Culloden and

each person contributed to his narrative as they were introduced. By the middle of his tale the old man had thrown down his rifle and seated himself next to them on the ground. He motioned for his son to follow his example. He was obviously much affected by the story and tears sprang several times to his eyes before Alasdair had finished.

There was silence for a moment. The old man looked at the ground, ashamed of himself. 'Please forgive my foolishness, yet you seemed such a suspicious group last night that I felt I had no choice. I sincerely hope that your heads are not too sore. I am Patrick Mackintosh. This is my son Alexander ... Alex, go and fetch what is left of the food and bring that bottle of whisky. Our guests,' Alasdair could not help smiling at the use of the word, 'must be hungry. My other son, John, is off hunting, for our food is almost gone.

'I too fought at Culloden with my brave boys. We ran south after the battle and hid for ten days before returning here to our village. Our family had been cruelly slaughtered. Everyone of them, down to the last child. I will not give you the details, for some of you have suffered in much the same way. We made graves for them ... ' He stopped for a moment in an attempt to control his emotions. 'Well, we have been here ever since. Two soldiers came a few days ago. They may have been deserters searching for loot, for they were very unkempt. We killed them. When we were returning from burying their bodies last night, we heard you talking and assumed that you too would find your way to our village. Can you blame us for being cautious?'

'Not at all, friend, not at all.' Alasdair answered.

Alex Mackintosh soon returned with meagre bowls of food and a bottle of whisky. The old man grabbed it from him as he passed.

'There is first one question I should like to ask before opening this beautiful bottle.'

'Ask away,' replied Jamie.

'Can myself and my sons join with you?'

'Join us?' Alasdair laughed. 'We should be delighted to have you ride with us. That must be the strongest arm in all the Highlands you possess there. I fear I will never breathe properly again.' He rubbed his neck and the crowd laughed heartily.

As Alexander Mackintosh passed around the barley cakes

119

and his father offered the bottle to each man in turn, Alasdair turned to MacLeish.

'Say, friend, you have not yet joined us officially. Would you like to?'

MacLeish thought for a few seconds. 'Is there a ceremony?'

'I am afraid that there is.'

'Then I'll join, for I do love ceremony.'

After they had drank and eaten, the men arose and joined their hands and muttered their oath.

Just as they finished, the sun came bursting forth and shone down on them, warming their backs.

Alasdair got down on his knees and asked them to join him in a short prayer for Lindsay Hamish. He sincerely hoped that it would be the last prayer he would have to speak for a member of the Clan.

Despite attempts on the part of the British officers to quieten rumours of the assasination attempt, the story was on the lips of everyone in Inverness on the morning after the event. Many a bottle of whisky was broken open and toasts not heard for many a week were whispered in glee, for the Jacobites in the town had precious little to cheer them during the days following the battle. It did not take long for the news to reach the jails, and the story caused a flutter of joy in the hearts of many men whose lives had seemed quite forlorn. Sporadic cheering had broken out in the cramped, dirty cellars, stopped only by violent beatings by the guards.

So crowed the supporters of the Prince. They had been right all along and a group of Highlanders had indeed risen in their darkest hour to bring them hope once more. The most astonishing part of the story for those who had known him well was MacLeish's involvement. Many of his merchant colleagues had shaken their heads in wonder to learn that people roused from their beds had seen their prominent citizen sprinting up Church Street with a rifle in his hand in hot pursuit of the mutilated officer who had recently excited so much comment. An investigation into the mystery of the waiting horses had revealed nothing. The people living in the close had had their homes turned upside down, but none would admit to having aided the renegades in any way.

An immediate tightening of security in the town had revealed some more Jacobite supporters, and the soldiers who had originally investigated MacLeish's loyalty were court-martialled. The rest of His Majesty's soldiers in the town became incorruptible overnight.

Only with Cumberland's exit to Fort Augustus did life begin to return to normal. The streets once more began to fill with dirt.

The Clan had postponed discussing their immediate plans until the return of John, Patrick Mackintosh's younger son, from his hunting. When he had recovered from his astonishment at seeing his father and brother surrounded by strangers, and had had the circumstances fully explained to him, he readily agreed to join with them. Unlike the other members of his family he had a quiet, kind face, but had inherited his father's brawny arms. Alasdair wondered, looking at him, whether such a peaceful-looking boy would be of any use in a fight.

Old Patrick Mackintosh caught him staring doubtfully at his son. 'Do not worry, MacDonald. He is fiercer and braver than any of us, and has the strength of ten cattle.'

Alasdair blushed with embarrassment and turned his attention to their immediate problems.

'Gentlemen,' he began. 'We now have to decide upon a course of action. I personally feel that, since our enterprise has failed and we have accomplished nothing so far we should carry on with the fight.'

'Aye,' Hugh agreed. 'I did not lose Lindsay just to give up now. His death has made me more determined than ever to pay these bastards back.'

Jamie, in contrast looked slightly doubtful, and Alasdair looked questioningly at him. 'Jamie, it is most unlike you not to relish a fight.'

The large Highlander's eyes flashed with rare anger at an imagined insult. 'It has nothing to do with that, and I will thank you not to suggest anything of the sort again. It is just that I feel it is time we thought of our families. Your wife, Hugh's wife . . . his sister,' (Hugh suppressed a wry smile), 'and my uncle. That young scoundrel Billy will have placed all their lives in jeopardy. We must consider their safety. Let us return and get them safely off to France, and then we can talk of continuing the struggle.'

Alasdair nodded thoughtfully. He had to admit to himself that it had not crossed his mind that Billy was now in a position to supply details of their personal lives, their homes, their friends and their families. Hinchcliffe would now know where to strike in order to cause the most damage.

He turned to the Mackintoshes. 'I realise that such considerations will not weigh heavily with you three who have just lost your whole family, and you have as much of a vote as the rest of us. Will you ride with us to save our kin?'

Patrick Mackintosh answered swiftly. 'The very fact that our dear family is dead makes us more aware of the necessity of protecting yours. Of course we will ride with you. There will be plenty of time for soldier-baiting after they have sailed.'

Everyone nodded in agreement, and Alasdair made a promise to himself that young Tom and John Mackintosh, who was not much older, would both be on that boat bound for safety. Too many young men had died already. He had been shocked and ashamed to see children no older than Angus lined up at Culloden to face the English.

'Very well. We must head towards Rannoch and Hugh's village. We will travel from there to Glencoe. Now, which way shall we travel?'

MacLeish spoke. 'Just before you came to Inverness I heard tell that Cumberland was to travel soon to Fort Augustus. The main routes will be crawling with soldiers if that were true.'

'Then we will have to travel by all the secret ways that we know.'

Patrick Mackintosh laughed. 'I realise that I do not have a pleasing shape, and that God must have been in humorous mood when he made me – I just thank him now that he did not play such pranks on my children's bodies – but these short legs have made me as sure as a goat in the mountains. I know many passes where man has never been before. As long as you can follow, I'll lead you safely to the west, and we'll travel by routes where we can take our horses.'

Within minutes they had set off and were trotting around the loch which Alasdair had smelt the night before. For once he was not leading the band, and was pleased to be able to relax, leaving MacLeish and Patrick Mackintosh to ride ahead, arguing keenly about routes.

For two days Hinchcliffe had scoured the countryside around Inverness searching for signs of his escaped prisoners. He had almost lost his mind under the strain of the search and had taken on the look of a hungry wolf. The image of Alasdair

MacDonald was always in his mind and he muttered constantly to himself as he searched for clues with his one good eye.

At length he came upon a village, which for no particular reason that he could put his finger on, aroused his suspicion. It stood next to a small loch. He rode in and dismounted and stood for a moment, senses alert, before making a hurried check inside each of the huts. There were signs of recent occupation. He returned to his horse and stood with its reins in his hand, every nerve in his body tingling. He spoke softly, bending to pick up an empty whisky bottle which lay at his feet. 'MacDonald, you were here. I feel it deep inside me, damn your eyes.' His low growl rose to a howling scream. 'DAMN YOUR EYES!' A hundred tiny animals flinched at the noise. He threw the empty bottle to the ground where it smashed. He wheeled his horse around, and jumping on to it, set off at a gallop for Inverness, a figure dressed entirely in black, riding a black horse. He was determined at all costs to be dressed correctly for Alasdair MacDonald's funeral.

Patrick Mackintosh had kept his promise. For two days the Clan had snaked and twisted its way through an extraordinary assortment of passes and crannies, now climbing so high that breathing became difficult, now plunging down hundreds of yards only to begin another climb immediately. They had passed under thundering waterfalls, disturbed startled eagles in their eyries, slipped on damp moss and waded through treacherous swamps. Each of them had received cuts and bruises on every part of their bodies and every limb ached.

In an attempt to keep their minds from their agonising pain and exhaustion, Patrick Mackintosh had talked almost continuously for forty-eight hours, recounting, it seemed, each minute detail of his life. By the evening of the second day, he had in his narrative, reached the age of forty. Alasdair estimated that they had at least twenty more years to suffer. Judging by the clarity of the old man's memory concerning his childhood Alasdair blanched at the prospect of reaching Glencoe without hearing the end of the story.

Interspersed amongst these details of his life were snatches of songs and a bewildering assortment of verses, poems and legends, many of which his travelling companions had never heard.

Interesting as these might have proved at a different time, as

123

the sun's rays disappeared over the top of the mountain they were climbing, Alasdair decided that they had suffered enough.

'Please, Patrick, silence for one moment.'

'But this story is particularly fascinating,' protested the old man.

'I am sure it is, and I am also sure that we have been fascinated by your personal history, but we are as tired as could be, the horses look as if they are ready to die, and I am just contemplating marching back to Inverness and giving myself up.'

'But this is what you wanted, MacDonald. We have not seen a living soul for two days. God himself would have found it difficult to follow the route that we have just traversed.' The old man sounded hurt.

'You have done your job excellently, believe me, but we must have sleep. Is there not an inn near here where we might eat in comfort before going onwards? Just to be out of the company of eagles for an hour would do us all a lot of good.'

'Very well. Just over this hill is a glen, there is an inn at the head of it which will provide shelter for a short while. But I warn you, we are taking a risk. We might run into soldiers and what then?'

'That,' said Alasdair, 'is a chance I am prepared to take at this moment.'

'It is your choice. Follow me.'

It took them nearly two hours to reach the top of the valley where the inn was situated. As they travelled up the glen, Alasdair felt a strong sensation of having been there before, but then he reflected, that was not so odd considering they had rejoined the major travelling routes. However, the feeling persisted and grew even stronger as they rode up to the inn from which, Alasdair noted with surprise, emanated pinpricks of light, giving it a ghostly quality against the night sky.

Patrick Mackintosh ordered them to stop some twenty yards from the building. Alasdair dismounted and walked ahead of his companions, feverishly searching his mind.

'Stand where you are.' He froze at the sound of the woman's voice.

'Come now,' Alasdair said, taking a step forward, 'this is no way to treat strangers.' The words were not out of his mouth when he heard the crack of a pistol shot followed instantly by a faint rush of air against his cheek where the ball had just missed him. The woman stood some five yards from him, her body outlined by the dim light from the inn.

124

Alasdair launched himself at her. A brief struggle ensued, during which he managed to knock the pistol from her grasp, and, when he had her sufficiently under control, dragged her towards the eerily-lit building while she kicked and scratched and swore at him. He pushed open the door, shoved her inside and followed close behind her.

Now all the strange feelings he had had coming up the valley were explained. Staring up at him from the floor where he had pushed her was the innkeeper's wife. Hugh was the next through the door. He gave a cry of astonishment at seeing the woman and rushed forwards to help her to her feet. She cringed at his approach and punched at his chest as he bent forward.

'Don't you recognise me? We are the men who saved you from the Englishman. Look, you must remember him.' Jamie had just walked through the door. Her eyes moved from one to the other of them. 'Of course,' she gasped. 'I am so sorry, but I have been so frightened. Oh, I cannot say how pleased I am to see you.'

Alasdair rushed forward and helped Hugh take her to the main table. When they had got her into a seat he noticed with shock the change that a few days had wrought in her face. Her eyes were circled with dark lines and the skin on her cheeks was stretched to reveal her cheekbones jutting obscenely through her flesh.

When the other members of the Clan had entered and had taken their seats round the table, Alasdair introduced them to the woman and bade her tell them what had happened since their departure. Their faces filled with admiration when they heard what she had done to the soldiers who had murdered her family.

When she had finished, Hugh spoke. 'We are deeply sorry to have brought such suffering upon your head.'

She smiled bravely. 'It is not your fault that the Devil is abroad in our land.'

'Why have you not left? You could have been miles from this place by now,' suggested Jamie.

She sighed heavily. 'I felt so hopeless without my husband and children. There seemed little point in carrying on. I decided to stay here and shoot some more of those murderers if they came this way. That is why I almost killed you, and I cannot begin to express my relief at not having done so. I did think of running away, but I really do not mind if I die now.

I have no reason to live.' She burst into tears and leant her cheek against the table surface. MacLeish moved round to her, put his arm around her shoulders and brought her head against his chest. The other Highlanders were silent for a moment in their sympathy until Hugh spoke.

'Alasdair, may I speak to you outside for a few seconds?'

Alasdair nodded and followed his companion to the outside of the house.

'Well, what is it?'

'Let's take her with us.'

'A woman, Hugh? Have you gone quite mad?'

'Aye, maybe I have, but I am talking about a woman who has killed five soldiers and has been waiting for the opportunity to kill more. Such a woman will hardly be trouble to us on our journey. We can put her on the boat to France with our own families. After all, we are partly responsible for what has happened to her, no matter how she tries to soothe our consciences.'

Alasdair turned away and thought for a while before replying.

'You're right. Let's go and ask her opinion. After all, she may not want to ride with us.' Inside, the other Clan members were wolfing down some food that had been placed before them. The innkeeper's wife bustled to and from the table, content at having something to do.

Alasdair waited until she had disappeared behind the partition into her living quarters before going to her.

'Pardon me one moment.' She looked up at him, obviously startled. 'Will you consent to accompany us on our journey? We will get you safe to France.' Hugh appeared from the next room and stood slightly behind Alasdair. 'Please do us the honour of accepting.'

She looked from one to the other of them and over the features of her face came an agonised expression born of happiness so acute, so sudden, it almost pained her.

She stumbled towards Hugh, sensing somehow that it had been his idea, and, placing her arms about him, buried her head in the folds of his plaid. 'Thank you, oh thank you. You have given me hope when I thought all was lost.'

Hugh turned towards the other room, holding her gently by the shoulders and took her to tell his fellow clan members the news.

CHAPTER THIRTEEN

THE KILLING

Eileen Gregor had found the days after Hugh's departure hard to bear. Her only comfort, as it had been during the months that Hugh had spent as a broken man on Rannoch, was his sister. Jeannie Gregor was as different from her brother as she was from Eileen. Hers was a happy nature, her demeanour cheerful and her spirits rarely anything but high, and her optimistic chatter had been a blessing at those moments when hope seemed to drain away from her sister-in-law.

They now sat opposite each other at the main table in the sitting room. Jeannie watched intently as Eileen attempted to thread a needle. Jeannie for once had given way to the despair that so rarely affected her. During the past few days only the thought of Jamie's return and of their future together had sustained her, but now her belief was in danger of weakening. She had never questioned that he would return. There seemed such a positive living force about the man that the thought of his death appeared ridiculous – but no more. The Clan had been gone for several days, and rumours concerning the murderous tactics of the English army spread daily. How could such a small band of men pit themselves against such mighty forces and expect to win? Why, even Prince Charlie had taken to his heels and was now, if the stories were to be believed, hiding among the Western Isles. And Hugh had worried her. There was about him an air of death, of impending doom that had been more pronounced than ever at their last meeting. And Alasdair MacDonald. In the eyes of that man there resided a madness. She had seen the desire for revenge many times in men's eyes – it had been that which had caused the downfall of her brother, the cause of his banishment to Rannoch – but in Alasdair it had taken on a different quality, an intensity that seemed unnatural, even in a Highlander.

Eileen sighed loudly and gave up trying to thread the needle.

Jeannie reached across and took it from her hand to attempt it herself. Eileen turned and stared bleakly out of the window to the back of the house. Jeannie thought of speaking, but realised that she had nothing left to give. It had all gone, evaporated with the coming of her own despair.

Strange, she reflected as she handed the threaded needle back, that people should so often maintain that successful marriages were made only between opposites. In many ways Eileen should have been Hugh's sister. Her wild, dark nature was so like his own and yet their marriage had been as perfect as any that Jeannie had known. They seemed to draw strength from their similarities, whereas it was the difference between them that bound Hugh and his quiet, trusting friend, Lindsay Hamish. She knew that Hugh had often plotted a marriage between the two of them, but although she liked Lindsay well enough, he had none of the qualities she loved instantly in Jamie – his joy, his laughter, his boyish innocence. It was her turn to sigh. Maybe Jamie would return after all. She wished it with all her heart.

A knock on the front door sounded throughout the house. Eileen looked up, startled. Jeannie carefully avoided her eyes, fearful of awakening there the hope that had begun to well in her own heart, rose from the table and moved quickly to the door.

Old McIan had spent the time since his nephew's departure in attempting to make up for the valuable farming time that had been lost to his Clan as a result of the conflict. His way of banishing dark thoughts of the future from his mind – and there had been many despite his speech to Alasdair – had been to throw himself body and soul into hard, gruelling work on the land, work that would have previously been thought undignified for one of his stature.

First, though, he had spared time to ferry the remaining women and children of his district to the Isle of Skye, sure in the knowledge that King George's vengeance would not stretch as far. As the days had passed, and there were still no signs of the army taking any retributive action against him, he had begun to feel a little foolish. After all, the army could gain nothing with such behaviour. Only a fool would believe that there was any possibility of another rebellion. No, the Highlanders, besides a few hotheads like his nephew and

Alasdair MacDonald, had been taught a lesson they would be unwise to forget. At first the men who had returned to the valley after Culloden had grumbled at his passive acceptance of defeat, but they had eventually followed his example and returned to their fields to salvage what they could. Their women and children had done well in their absence – for they were the main work-force in times of peace – and there was a chance that with a little application, they would not starve in the winter months.

A few of the men had kept their wives by their side, and some had left with them to travel across the water, but there were few women in the valley, and the only one that did not have her husband with her was Kathy. McIan had pleaded, cajoled and finally shouted at her, but in the end did not have the courage to use his strongest argument against her. He could not bring himself to suggest that there was little, if any, hope of her husband and his nephew returning. They had been gone too long and had more than likely been cut down in some rash action against the redcoats, or were now languishing in some jail. He did not much like to face the thought himself, for his fondness for his nephew, clumsy and irritatingly boisterous as he had often been, was great and he had missed him badly since his departure.

It was late in the evening, and his every limb ached in a most satisfying way. He had idly considered carrying on with this mode of life after the cessation of the troubles. Beads of perspiration which had formed along his eyebrows dropped on to his cheeks as he stood upright and prepared to return to the house. He had taken but a few steps towards his home when he heard hoofbeats. He dropped his spade and searched in his pockets for a handkerchief with which to wipe away the sweat. When he had wiped his face he looked up, but could only see the approaching riders dimly as they rode, black shadows, out of the setting sun.

The journey across the country had been arduous for the Clan. Hugh, Alasdair and Jamie had been able to relieve Patrick Mackintosh of the responsibility for finding out-of-the-way routes, for they all knew the western part of the country better than he. They had also been spared listening to the old man's story, for MacLeish had taken it upon himself to keep them amused with tales concerning the travels he

9   129

had undertaken in strange countries in support of his trade. Even for Jamie and Alasdair, who had both seen a part of Europe, the stories were enthralling, and Tom and young John Mackintosh had found much of the narrative difficult to believe, so large a portion of their lives having passed within a few miles of their birthplace. The greater part of his story had concerned a year spent in the New World, a land of plenty where crops grew extraordinarily quickly, and where people of different beliefs and customs could live together in harmony, and fierce, red-skinned natives roamed the country almost naked. MacLeish had already decided to leave once more for those wild shores when his present adventure had ended. From the gleam of excitement he had noticed in John Mackintosh's eyes when he had mentioned his plans, he guessed that he would have a young travelling companion with him when he arrived in Boston.

He was in the middle of describing the black natives who were used as slaves in the fields, when Hugh Gregor's home came into view. Hugh raised himself in his saddle and shouted excitedly, pointing it out to his companions. Despite their desperate tiredness, they galloped for the final few hundred yards and clattered to a halt. At the front door of his home, Hugh leapt from his horse and burst inside, the rest of the Clan on his heels. He gave a cry of deep anguish and froze in his steps. Alasdair walked past him into the main room to see what had so upset his friend.

There in the middle of the floor, was Jeannie on her knees, rocking backwards and forwards, wringing her hands. Stretched out beside her was Eileen. An ugly red stain marred the whiteness of her dress. Her face stared up at Alasdair, a strange, peaceful look in her unseeing eyes. Alasdair, thinking quickly, turned to Hugh, and taking him roughly by the shoulders, pushed him out of the house and made him sit on the ground. The Highlander, normally so strong and cynical, sat howling like a lost child, his fists pressed against his temples as if he were trying to force the memory of what he had just seen from his mind.

A feeling of guilt rose in Alasdair's breast, for whichever way he looked at it, he had been responsible for this. True, if it had not been for him, Hugh might still have been stranded on Rannoch, but at least he would have had Lindsay Hamish as a companion, and would have been safe in the knowledge that his wife still lived. Now he was bereft of everything. His best friend, his wife, many members of his clan, all lay dead on account of Alasdair's desire for revenge. Alasdair felt a tap on his shoulder and looked round to find the innkeeper's wife standing beside him. He realised that he did not even know her name. She pointed towards the house, indicating that Alasdair should return.

As he walked away she sat by Hugh and tenderly drew his head to her breast and began gently stroking his hair. They had both suffered much and she needed him as much as he needed her. Inside the house all was quiet. The body of Hugh's wife had been covered with a sheet, and the Clan members were standing uncomfortably around the central table of the room. The only one who had sat down was Jamie, who had his arm around Jeannie's shoulders. She had stopped crying and her red-rimmed eyes stared dully in front of her.

Alasdair noticed an ugly black bruise on her forehead. 'Please tell us what happened,' he asked quietly.

She turned her gaze upon him slowly, and drawing a handkerchief from a pocket of her skirt, wiped her face before replying. 'There was a knock at the door and I ran to it, thinking you had all returned. When I opened it, however, there was a man standing there the like of whom I have never seen before. He was dressed all in black, with a black patch across his eye. One of his ears was mutilated. He grinned at me most horribly and asked if I was Eileen Gregor. I told him no and asked him who he might be. He laughed at me. It sounded crazy, like a madman's laugh. I saw something in his hand which he swung at me and I fell to the floor. I dimly remember hearing a loud explosion. It must have been the pistol that killed . . . ' She stopped for a moment, unable to continue. Jamie patted her gently on the back and she began again 'It happened about an hour ago. I cannot remember more.' She paused. 'Tell me, who was he? He looked as if he had come straight from Hell itself.'

'Aye, and we'll send him back there as soon as we catch him,' snarled Jamie.

It took about an hour for the Clan to go around the members of the village asking each of them if they wished to journey to France. Surprisingly few accepted, and they ended up with only one old man and two old women. When they had all gathered in the main house, Alasdair raised his hand to hush the general conversation. In the ensuing silence they could hear Hugh's steady sobs from the next room where the inn-keeper's wife was still comforting him. Alasdair spoke. 'You have a few hours to pack your belongings and get ready to leave. We shall be travelling first to Glencoe to collect my wife and any of the people there who wish to come with us. I hope for his sake that McIan has already sent the women and children away. From there we will travel to the coast. I know of many good men who will ferry us across to Ireland. You can either stay there where there is a chance that the English might follow or you can travel on to France, which is my recommendation. Once there you will be safe, for Louis will protect you. Some of us will be staying behind. We will not make any decisions here. During the next two hours Jamie, MacLeish, Tom and Alexander will scout the moor with me to see if we can spot the murderer. Do not waste any time. I suggest you try and convince the other people in the village to follow your wise example. If they want convincing of their likely fate if they remain, then bring them in here to see the body of Hugh's wife. That, my friends, is the quality of the Englishmen's mercy.'

He moved quickly to the door and waited outside for the men he had called to appear. To his surprise, Patrick Mackintosh joined the party with his youngest son John, even though neither of them had been mentioned. The afternoon sun was warm and Alasdair could feel the sweat forming on his brow.

'Patrick and John, I did not call you. What are you doing out here?'

The old man replied. 'You accept us into your Clan, telling us that we are to revenge ourselves on the English, and then you leave us behind as soon as the fun starts. You must think us very poor specimens.'

'I was just wishing to protect your family. If something happens to us on this ride, there will be no one left to carry on your name.'

The old man hoisted his short legs across the broad back of his sturdy horse.

'If we cannot ride the Highlands with honour then there seems little point in carrying my name.' Alasdair smiled as he levered himself on to his own horse. He checked about him to make sure that everyone had come out. Only Jamie was missing. He could just make out his huge friend through the window of the house. The Highlander stood embracing Jeannie.

'I realise that this is not the time to ask you, but did you receive my ring?'

She nodded.

'And my letter?'

She nodded again, a sad smile on her lips.

'And have you thought about what I said while I was away?'

'About nothing else.' She paused for a moment. 'And I will be delighted to have you as my husband. At least one good thing will have come out of all this suffering.'

They kissed quickly, and then Jamie opened the door and ran to his horse without looking back.

'Glad you could come,' Alasdair greeted him. They turned their horses round and sped off across the Moor.

They had ridden hard for an hour with no sign of their quarry and Alasdair was just about to give the signal for their return when he heard a horse whinney. The sound came from some distance away. He brought his men to a halt and stood in his saddle, shielding his eyes against the sun in order to look about him. A peregrine falcon hovered lazily on currents of air, but nothing else moved and all was silent once more in the drowsy evening sun. He settled himself back in his saddle and was about to go on when he heard the noise once more, only louder this time.

'What was that?' asked Jamie, riding some ten yards behind. So Alasdair had not been mistaken.

They were heading towards a small hill, a gentle bump in the Moor's flat surface. The only possible source of the sound was from beyond its crest. Alasdair signalled for the others to wait, dropped from his horse and crawled on his stomach to the top of the hillock and peered over.

Some 200 yards in the distance ten riders snaked forward in single file. With a start Alasdair realised they were soldiers escorting Highland prisoners. The first of the bound horsemen had flaming white hair and a beard to match and it was his horse that snorted and whinnied, obviously unused to being ridden without the tug of reins to guide it. The rider was old McIan. No sooner had Alasdair recognised the proud erect figure of his Chief than something else caught his eye. It was another rider galloping in from the other direction. Even at that distance the man looked odd. Alasdair strained his eyes to make him out. The new rider, like the horse he rode, was

133

dressed entirely in black. He remembered how Jeannie had described Eileen's murderer. They had found Hinchcliffe after all.

Alasdair watched in fascinated horror as the black horse reached the leader of the column which had now stopped. The soldier listened for a moment to Hinchcliffe, shook his head violently and waved him aside.

Hinchcliffe reached into his coat pocket and brought forth a piece of paper which he handed to the redcoat. The soldier read it quickly and sat up straight in his saddle with a jerk, saluted Hinchcliffe sharply and turned to shout an order. Two of the soldiers at the back of the line leapt from their horses and running to either side of McIan pulled him unceremoniously from his steed.

Hinchcliffe got down slowly from his horse, and walking towards the group, motioned for the two soldiers to stand away He bent and pulled the old man to his knees, and then appeared to speak for nearly a minute. When he had finished he cocked his head on one side, an action which Alasdair remembered with a shiver from their last meeting. The Captain was waiting for a reply. Getting no response he lashed at McIan's head. The old man fell over on to the ground. Hinchcliffe pounced on him and shook him by the collar, banging his head repeatedly against the earth.

Alasdair leapt to his feet, much to the astonishment of the rest of the Devil's Clan who had been watching him with curiosity for some minutes, ignorant of events beyond the hill.

He drew his sword and waved it vigorously above his head and bellowed across the Moor.

'Hinchcliffe, you stinking son of a mango-ridden cur. You have been looking for me. Well, here I am, all alone. Come for me, if you have the guts!' He leapt down from the hillock and ran to the other Highlanders and spoke hurriedly to them.

'All right men, off your horses, quickly. Climb to the top of the hill, but don't show your heads above it. There must be seven men heading for us at the moment. Six redcoats and a certain officer you will have no difficulty in recognising. We will leap up at the last moment, just as they clear the ridge. The surprise alone should kill them. Come on, hurry!' They could already hear the sound of the horses' hooves pounding towards them, and suppressing the urge to whoop and yell as would have befitted their entry into battle, the men leapt from their horses and crawled quickly to just below the crest of the ridge.

Alasdair stayed behind to shoo the horses away and then scrambled up the hill and flung himself down beside Jamie. Their faces were pressed hard against the soft moss.

'Jamie, not that you'll need any spur to fight, but I had better warn you that your father and some of your family are prisoners over the ridge. If we win, we can release them.' Jamie's eyes, astonished at first, narrowed into slits of hatred and resolve.

The first horse was on them quicker than they had bargained for. It was Hinchcliffe's black mare. He had hit the other side of the ridge at such a speed that he sailed over the heads of the Highlanders, safely out of reach. The next horse had approached more slowly, and as it leapt over the top, Jamie plunged his sword straight into its soft underbelly. The horse shrieked and tumbled forward, crushing its rider to death as it plummeted to the bottom of the hillock. The next five horses had approached in line, and the Highlanders stood in unison to greet them, their swords plunging and scything into the animals and their riders as they flew past. One of the horses caught Alexander Mackintosh full in the chest and killed him instantly. His father turned and raced down the slope to where the rider was scrambling to his feet and chopped his sword into the back of the man's exposed neck.

The encounter was over in seconds. Alasdair looked frantically around to see what had become of Hinchcliffe but there was no sign of him. He looked up to see Jamie straddling the hillock, frozen in an attitude of horror. Alasdair ran to his side and followed his gaze.

There, thundering along at great speed, was Hinchcliffe. His hat flew into the air behind him as he galloped. He was rapidly approaching the prisoners who still sat on their horses, powerless to move. In desperation, when it looked as though Hinchcliffe might collide with them, they began spurring their mounts to get out of his way. When they had moved, Alasdair and Jamie could see something directly in the crazed Captain's path. It was old McIan, who still lay on the ground, recovering from his recent beating. As Hinchcliffe approached him, he slowed his horse and the Highlanders could see a sword gleaming in his hand, cruel and cold in the evening sun. The old man had crawled to his knees and was now crouched, staring up in horror at the Angel of Death. As he passed the old man,

Hinchcliffe took careful aim, bent low in his saddle and brought the sword crashing into McIan's neck. The old man screamed and blood spurted into the air from a severed artery. He remained crouching for a moment, his mouth wide open, eyes staring sightlessly ahead, and then sinking to his knees he crumpled to the ground. The Highlanders could hear the sound of high-pitched, inhuman laughter coming to them from across the Moor.

It took them some minutes to round up the horses and then the Clan rode to the captive Highlanders. Jamie jumped from his horse and knelt praying by the body of his uncle, while Alasdair listened to an account of events by the three other members of McIan's family who were also being taken to Fort Augustus to receive justice directly at the hands of Cumberland.

The troops, it appeared, had taken them by surprise as they toiled in the fields, and yet, despite the speed of the attack, many of their companions had managed to escape. When Alasdair asked for news of his wife they shrugged, for none of them had seen her prior to the attack. Alasdair masked his disappointment at the lack of news as they thanked him profusely for saving their lives. The enthusiasm of their gratitude was aided by the fact that none of them had been particularly kind to members of Alasdair's village in the past, but Alasdair was not thinking of that as the three of them went to attend to the body of their dead Chief. While the three clansmen followed Jamie, who had the body of his leader slung in front of him across his horse back to Glencoe, Alasdair and the rest of the Clan retraced their steps to Hugh's house with an equally distressing burden, the body of Alexander Mackintosh, carried fittingly by one of the redcoat's horses.

CHAPTER FOURTEEN

THE DECISION

Several members of Hugh's village had joined the three old people who had originally accepted the invitation to travel to France by the time that the Clan had reached his house. Hugh Gregor, his face a tortured mask, stood rather unsteadily between Jeannie and the innkeeper's wife. The journey back from Rannoch had been a silent one in the main. Alasdair had tried to apologise to Patrick for the loss of his son, and the old man, his face tired and grey after the aftermath of the ordeal, had seemed to accept his words of condolence. Alasdair had suggested that they bury Alexander's body in the Gregor burial ground and the old man accepted without comment.

Two short, heart-rending ceremonies were performed and when Eileen Gregor and Alexander Mackintosh had been laid to rest, the party mounted their horses and headed wearily for Glencoe.

It was a long and tiring ride and their progress was slowed by the old people they had agreed to bring with them and by the necessity of keeping out of the way of any patrols that might be traversing the Moor.

Throughout their journey Alasdair kept asking himself whether it had all been worth it, and if the personal grief of his companions could be justified by his own need for revenge. As a terrible feeling of guilt afflicted him, he remembered the words of Patrick Mackintosh. 'If we cannot ride the Highlands with honour, then there seems little point in carrying on my name.' Yes, perhaps that was where the justification for all this misery lay. And then he remembered the body of his son Angus, and his dying father and the words of old McIan and his talk of compromise, and realised that the word, the very concept made him feel sick to the pit of his stomach. Even if Kathy were dead when he arrived at Glencoe – and nothing that happened to him or his friends could equal that tragedy – he would not question his actions further. What he was doing had to be done. The rightness of it all could be felt in his veins. A

Highlander without his land, a warrior without his honour. What life was there in such an existence?

He hoped that his friends would realise the truth of that, for if they did not, then they had truly lost everything.

At length, on the morning of the second day of their journey, they entered Glencoe. Alasdair smiled up at the glowering black mountains, and the melancholy disposition of the valley cheered him immensely, but no sooner had his mood begun to lighten than his village came in sight. He averted his eyes hurriedly. John Mackintosh, his age an excuse for his ignorance, leant across to Alasdair as they passed the crude huts.

'Might there not be someone there who is in need of our help?'

'No. There is no one,' murmured Alasdair.

'How do you know?'

'It is my village.'

The boy settled himself back in his saddle, his face burning with shame and embarrassment.

Alasdair looked at him out of the corner of his eye and summoned a pale smile. 'Do not worry, young friend. You were not to know and it was kind of you to ask.'

The boy smiled with gratitude.

They rode on in silence.

All the way along the valley Alasdair felt as though they were being spied upon, yet every time he turned to look about and behind him, there was nothing. Once or twice he fancied seeing a shape out of the corner of his eye, but no matter how fast he turned he could not place it. The irritating sensation persisted right up until they reached McIan's house at the head of the valley. Alasdair climbed wearily from his horse, a feeling of dread in his heart, for he had been expecting to see Kathy run from the house to greet him. Could she really be dead after all they had been through, he wondered? He felt unwilling to approach the house.

The sound of laughter broke into his gloomy thoughts. It had come from the back of the house and he stepped forward to investigate, only to come face to face with a young red-coated soldier rushing around the side of the building. Each member of the Clan dived for his pistol and the boy would undoubtedly have died had Jamie not appeared behind him an instant later.

He cried in horror at the scene which met his eyes. 'Good God, my friends, this is no redcoat. It's one of my cousins we rescued on the Moor.' Alasdair almost cried with relief.

The boy looked abashed.

'I'm so sorry, gentlemen, I did not do it on purpose. I could not think of a less humorous joke. The soldiers must have missed one of their dead when they came for us originally, and I was merely trying on his clothes. They might come in useful for one of your daring schemes, Alasdair.'

Alasdair dismissed the boy with a wave of his hand and turned to Jamie.

'My dear friend, I am almost feared to ask you, but . . . '

'Do not fret, man, she is safe. She is at the back of the house being wooed by the other boys. I think that they are almost hoping that you do not return.' He laughed as Alasdair scampered past him. She was sitting on a splendidly coloured shawl some fifty yards from the house. He sprinted to her side and they embraced passionately, while the young men who had been keeping her company discreetly moved away from the touching scene.

'Oh, Kathy darling, I was so worried. How in heaven's name did you escape the soldiers?'

'I was downstairs in the main room when I heard them approach. I ran to the window to see who was there, hoping with all my heart that it was you, and when I saw that I could do nothing, hid behind the panel which hides a secret room next to the fireplace. I hid in there, trembling with fear, for maybe twelve hours before creeping out to search the house. Everyone had gone, including the soldiers. I returned to my hiding place in case the soldiers returned and have spent most of the time there until Jamie's return. I could hardly believe my ears when I heard his voice.'

'You are a clever woman. I was never so happy to see anyone.'

'Nor I, dearest husband.'

They walked, their arms around each other's waists, to the front of the house where a not dissimilar scene had just taken place between Jamie and Jeannie.

On the next morning they gathered in the main room. The previous day had been spent in celebrating and commiserating, remembering and honouring, chattering and loving. The assembled company looked eagerly at Alasdair when he called for silence.

'We must leave for the coast where we will get a boat. There are ferrymen who have served the MacDonalds of Glencoe and will be happy to do us this service. One of them will take those of us who are bound for France to Ireland. He will then put you in touch with a captain who will take you onwards from there.'

'It is already arranged, Alasdair. The ferryman is waiting for us now. Old Andrew it is, whom I have known since birth.'

'He is one of the very best. Good work, Jamie. Now what about money? I fear that I have little left to help you on your journey, although I have enough for Kathy and for one other.'

Jamie spoke again. 'Our coffers are fairly full. My dear uncle was a canny man and hid gold at the start of the troubles. As you well know, he never believed that we had any chance of success. There is enough there to pay for all of us to get to France and enough to live on comfortably for upwards of a year with no further income.'

Alasdair smiled. 'It appears that all my work has been done for me. There is only one question that remains to be asked.'

'Who is going?' asked Hugh abruptly. It was the first time he had spoken since his wife's death. It worried Alasdair. Did this mean that Hugh, upon whose strong shoulders was so much reliance, was prepared to give up the fight? Not that Alasdair would have blamed him in the least. He had borne all that could be expected of a man, but it would be a sad and bitter disappointment to him nevertheless.

'Anyone who wishes, Hugh. Do you intend going yourself?'

'My only interest is that Jeannie should go. As for myself, we shall see.'

'Hugh!' She jumped to her feet. 'I shall be staying here with you and Jamie where I belong.'

Hugh looked at her and his eyes clouded with sorrow.

'Jeannie, my dear, discounting for a moment my brave companions here, you are the only thing I have left. I have lost my wife and my best friend. Will you not consent to do this one thing for me? If I did not have you to return to, what would be the point of my carrying on?'

Jeannie's lips trembled. She moved across to her brother and hugged him. 'You know I would do anything for you, dear Hugh. The only thing I ask for in return is guarantee of your safety.' She turned to face the assembled company. 'Why do any of us have to stay behind in this sorry land? Have we not all suffered enough already? There is not one of us in this room who has not lost someone dear to them in the past few weeks. We have given our all for the Highlands. What else have we to give?'

Hugh turned away from her and stared from the window to the fields up the Glen. Alasdair glanced at Kathy who began shaking her head and walked over to Jeannie's side.

'My dear Miss Gregor, your arguments are sound. God knows I have rehearsed them often enough in my own mind recently. But these are menfolk you are dealing with.' She smiled and took hold of Jeannie's hands.

'They do not have our logic for all that they might say about us, and there is nothing we can do about that. I do not suggest that we support them in everything they do, but at times such as these when their decisions are difficult and their minds are tortured, we must stand by them. Alasdair has asked me to leave for France without him. Whether he will survive to join me there I do not know, but I would rather that if he stayed, he stayed with my blessing. Can you not do the same for Hugh should he decide against leaving? I am asking a lot of you, but I think from the little I know of you that you are a person used to giving.'

Jeannie looked slowly from Hugh to Jamie and then into Kathy's eyes. She stared into them for almost a minute before nodding her head slowly in acquiescence.

Alasdair broke the ensuing silence. 'Thank you, dear wife.' He loved her more dearly at that moment, for her patience and her seemingly infinite understanding, than he had ever done. 'I see that it was wrong to bring up this subject here. Far better that we should leave such decisions until the last moment. Everyone can think about it while we journey to the boat.' He stared briefly at Tom. He promised himself that the boy would leave on the same boat as his wife. The youth had taken on a gaunt, haunted expression during the past weeks and lines of exhaustion were clearly etched in his face. The child had suffered enough. Alasdair would not let him die like Angus. It would have been like losing a son twice over, and no man could bear such a thing.

'When do you propose that we leave?' asked Jamie.

'At once, my friend.' He quelled the hubbub that his remark occasioned amongst the people gathered in the room by raising his hand. 'While travelling down the Glen yesterday, I felt someone watching me, and judging from my reaction, their gaze was not well-intentioned.'

'I felt it too,' MacLeish agreed.

'Good, so I am not going mad at least. There might be a party of soldiers descending on us at this moment. I was frightened in case they attacked during the night, but realised that none of us was ready to travel yesterday. Now we must make haste.'

It took them the better part of an hour to prepare themselves for the journey. No sooner had they gone a mile from the house than they turned to see spirals of smoke ascending from the proud old building that had for so long housed the Chiefs of the MacDonalds of Glencoe. As the first flames started to lick through the lower windows, Alasdair turned his gaze away, never to look back. Since that day, fifty years before, when the Campbells had turned villainously upon their hosts, murdering everyone upon whom they could lay their hands, the valley had not seen a darker day.

The party stood by the water's edge in the small cove, staring at the large, sturdy boat that was to take them to Ireland. The ferryman sat patiently on the shingle, puffing on a pipe and gazing wistfully across the water, which billowed and swelled with the strong wind blowing towards Ireland's shore.

'Well,' began Alasdair, 'who shall go and who shall stay? You have all had time to make up your minds.'

The people from Hugh's village murmured their intention to leave, and Jeannie, a reluctant look in her eye, nodded.

There was an awkward silence.

MacLeish spoke. 'I am afraid that I shall be leaving as well. This is no place for us now. We should look towards the New World for our future. I intend returning to America. Alasdair, I know you have things to settle here, and I wish you all the good fortune in the world. For the rest of my life I shall remember you and be proud to think that I was once a companion of all you brave, brave people, and I will, I promise, always be a member of the Devil's Clan.'

Alasdair stepped forward and shook his old friend warmly by the hand. He could find no words to express the affection he felt for him and so remained silent.

The innkeeper's wife stared imploringly at MacLeish.

'Sir, I know that I'm being impertinent, but I should be most happy if you would consent to let me accompany you. There is no reason for me stay here.'

'My dear lady, you may travel with me as an equal. I shall be delighted. And what about you, my young friend. I saw a look in your eyes when I spoke of my foreign adventures that suggested a more than passing interest on your part.' He turned to young John Mackintosh.

A light blazed for a moment in the boy's eyes before he stared meekly down at the ground. 'I shall do whatever my father tells me.'

Patrick Mackintosh stared at the boy for a while, a struggle taking place in his own mind. The boy looked up at him and suddenly burst forth. 'Father, let us go there. It will be a new life for us, and there will be new mountains for you to climb. Mr MacLeish has told me so. If we leave, we may at least have a chance to forget the past.'

The old man's eyes glazed over and his chin trembled with emotion. 'The past, my son, is not so easy to forget, I assure you. There would be no point in my starting a new life at my age, and these mountains have suited me well in the past and will suit me well enough in the future.'

The boy looked crestfallen. 'But you, my dear son, you must go. This is no country for young people. Mr MacLeish here is a good man, one of the best I have met in a long life. You will do well with him'. The boy rushed towards him. 'No, leave me now. Farewells would only make me cry, and that is not something I wish to do in front of my son. Good luck, my boy. I have been more proud of you than I can say.' He turned away and walked down to the water. Alasdair restrained John from following him.

'No, John,' he whispered in his ear. 'This is the way he wishes it to be. Grant his request.'

'And you, you three rascals, you will be leaving as well,' said Jamie turning to his young cousins. 'No. Do not argue with me. Now that old McIan, God rest his soul, is gone, you are under my care. I intend to have some members of my family left alive when I am dead.' The boys nodded, not wishing to raise his ire.

'And you, Tom?' asked Alasdair.

'I stay with you, of course.'

'No, boy. I was hoping you might make the right decision, but I will have to make it for you, I see that. I will not ask one so young to court death any longer. You have been like a son to

143

me. Do me the honour of obeying me now as if you were one.'
He turned quickly to avoid seeing the tears of supplication that
had sprung to the boy's eyes.

He turned to Hugh. 'You need not ask me, Alasdair. I cannot
leave now. There is much to do before my heart and conscience
can be at peace again. I ride with you.'

Alasdair's heart leapt with joy. To have lost Hugh as well
would have been like forsaking a wife, a son and brother at the
same time. 'Thank you, Hugh,' he whispered, 'you do not know
what that means to me.' It took some fifteen minutes to load
everything on to the boat. Alasdair had already said his good-
byes to Kathy on the previous evening, and Jamie kept his part-
ing from Jeannie as short as possible.

'When next I see you, darling woman, we shall be wed. That is
a promise,' he whispered as he helped her on to the boat.

The four remaining men pushed the boat away from the
shore into the billowing waves and then stood silent, water lap-
ping at their feet, the unspeakable ache of loneliness spreading
through them, for each had said goodbye to something he truly
loved.

As the boat, aided by the wind, sped towards the vacant line
between the angry sea and the grey, threatening sky, the men
began to mutter prayers. The soft pleas were torn from their
mouths by the wind and carried heavenwards.

When the boat had disappeared from view, they turned and
walked away, the shingle crunching under their feet. They had
got almost halfway to the face of the cliff which overlooked the
cove when a strange sensation caused Alasdair to look round.
Emerging from the sea, weed tangled on his wet clothing, hair
plastered across his face, mouth wide open gasping for breath,
stood Tom.

He staggered up the beach to Alasdair and fell forwards into
his arms. The tears which Alasdair had been controlling for so
long started to flood as he held the young boy to his breast. It
was almost as if his son had been returned to him.

'Look up there,' cried Jamie. Alasdair dried his eyes and
turned to follow his companion's pointing finger.

At the top of the cliff face, staring down at them, was a figure
on a horse. They were both motionless. A man dressed entirely
in black, atop a black steed. An Angel of Death. The Highlanders felt a wave of menacing evil wash over them.

'Come, friends,' growled Alasdair. 'We have debts to collect.'